Glimpses of the Moon

A Jazz Age Musical

Book & Lyrics by Tajlei Levis

Music by John Mercurio

Based on the Novel by
Edith Wharton

A SAMUEL FRENCH ACTING EDITION

SAMUEL FRENCH

FOUNDED 1830

NEW YORK HOLLYWOOD LONDON TORONTO

SAMUELFRENCH.COM

ISBN 978-0-573-69905-4   Printed in U.S.A.   #29718

RENTAL MATERIALS

An orchestration consisting of **Piano, One Multiple Reed (flute, clarinet, alto sax, optional oboe), Bass, Drum, and Vocal Score** will be loaned two months prior to the production ONLY on the receipt of the Licensing Fee quoted for all performances, the rental fee and a refundable deposit.

Please contact Samuel French for perusal of the music materials as well as a performance license application.

IMPORTANT BILLING AND CREDIT
REQUIREMENTS

All producers of *GLIMPSES OF THE MOON* must give credit to the Authors of the Play in all programs distributed in connection with performances of the Play, and in all instances in which the title of the Play appears for the purposes of advertising, publicizing or otherwise exploiting the Play and/or a production. The name of the Authors *must* appear on a separate line on which no other name appears, immediately following the title and *must* appear in size of type not less than fifty percent of the size of the title type.

In addition the following credit *must* be given in all programs and publicity information distributed in association with this piece:

GLIMPSES OF THE MOON
Based on the Novel by Edith Wharton
Book and Lyrics by Tajlei Levis   Music by John Mercurio

GLIMPSES OF THE MOON opened at the Oak Room of New York City's literary landmark Algonquin Hotel on January 21, 2008 in a production directed by Marc Bruni, choreographed by Denis Jones, with musical direction by John Mercurio and produced by Lemon Tree Productions. The production featured costumes by Lisa Zinni, lighting designed by Jim Milkey, scenic design by Ted LeFevre, and casting by Geoff Josselson. The cast was as follows:

SUSY BRANCH . . . . Patti Murin
ELLIE VANDERLYN. . . . . .Beth Glover
NELSON VANDERLYN . . . . .Daren Kelly
URSULA GILLOW/CORAL HICKS/MAID . . . . .Laura Jordan
WINTHROP "STREFFY" STREFFORD . . . . Glenn Peters
NICK LANSING. . . . . Stephen Plunkett
CABARET SINGER . . . . Liz Larsen

GLIMPSES OF THE MOON returned to the Oak Room on October 26, 2008 in an extended run produced by Sharon Carr and Associates, with the same creative team plus musical direction by Rick Hip-Flores. The Equity Stage Manager was Carlos Maisonet. The cast was as follows:

SUSY BRANCH . . . . .Autumn Hurlbert
ELLIE VANDERLYN. . . . . Jane Blass
NELSON VANDERLYN . . . . .Daren Kelly
URSULA GILLOW/CORAL HICKS/MAID . . . . .Laura Jordan
WINTHROP STREFFY. . . . . Glenn Peters
NICK LANSING. . . . . Chris Peluso
CABARET SINGER . . . . Liz Larsen

Producing Artistic Director Carolyn Griffin presented the theatrical premiere of *GLIMPSES OF THE MOON* at MetroStage in Alexandria, Virginia on September 10, 2010 in a production directed and choreographed by David Marquez, with musical direction by Darius Smith, costumes designed by Lisa Zinni, lighting by Andrew F. Griffin and scenic design by Daniel Pinha. The Equity Stage Manager was Jessica Winfield. The cast was as follows:

SUSY BRANCH . . . . .Natascia Diaz
ELLIE VANDERLYN. . . . . Gia Mora
NELSON VANDERLYN . . . . Stephen F. Schmidt
URSULA GILLOW/CORAL HICKS/MAID . . . . Lauren "Coco" Cohn*
WINTHROP STREFFY. . . . . .Matthew A. Anderson
NICK LANSING. . . . . Sam Ludwig
CABARET SINGER . . . . Lori Williams/Roz White/Tracy McMullan

* nominated for Helen Hayes Award: Outstanding Supporting Actress in a Resident Musical

CHARACTERS

SUSY BRANCH (late 20s) – Susy is bright, pretty and practical. Though born into society, her father's gambling habit and untimely death left her dependent on wealthy friends who appreciate her grace, charm, and enthusiasm.

WINTHROP "STREFFY" STREFFORD (30-50) – Streffy is British and proper, fourth in line to inherit a title and large fortune. In the meantime, he is a career freeloader, dining out on rich Americans' fondness for European royalty. Though gossipy, selfish and a bit mean, he is fun to have around. He has long been secretly in love with Susy, but being too poor to have any chance to marry, he has settled for being her friend and confidante.

ELLIE VANDERLYN (late 40s) – Self-absorbed wealthy society matron. She is attractive, ambitious, self-centered, used to getting whatever she likes.

NELSON VANDERLYN (50-60) – Successful banker, he has endured 20 years of marriage to Ellie. And somehow, despite her mistreatment, remains steadfastly in love with her.

URSULA GILLOW (late 40s) – A vain society matron, even richer than the Vanderlyns. She and Ellie have a longstanding rivalry. (The same actor plays Coral, below.)

NICK LANSING (30s) – A scholar of classical archeology who dreams of writing historical novels, Nick is romantic and passionate, well-traveled, curious. He appreciates beauty and the finer things, but has an old fashioned moral strength. He had a small inheritance but burned through it quickly several years earlier. Like Susy, he was born rich to a good family, went to the right schools and clubs, but is now without sufficient funds.

CORAL HICKS (20s) – Frowsy over-educated heiress from the Midwest. Her father founded a successful department store. She is serious, awkward, overly intellectual but socially inept. She knows everything in books and nothing about human interaction. This actor will also play Ursula and a Maid.

MAID – Female (20-40). A servant at the Vanderlyn's Newport mansion.

THE CABARET SINGER – 40s-70s. This is a guest-starring part with a one-song walk-on and a few lines, requiring minimal preparation. Ideally, each week of the run could feature a different 'name' performer in this role. (It is also possible to have the actor who plays Ellie perform this role.)

SETTING

The Vanderlyns' Manhattan Brownstone and Newport Mansion, and other places where society plays.

TIME

The action takes place over the course of a year, from April 1922 to April 1923.

A NOTE FROM THE DIRECTOR

This show is a sparkling romance, a comedy of manners, a social satire of the upper classes. Though it is only a few years after some of Wharton's Edwardian tragedies, *Glimpses of the Moon* takes place in a rapidly changing world. The stock market is high, the newly rich are starting to break through society, women have the vote, the corsets are gone, advertising is in, the music is jazzier, the dancing more frenetic. Despite all these freedoms, the characters are still pressured by convention and forced to make choices. Fundamentally, this show explores how they choose between love and money.

The idea of running out of time has great importance to each of the characters, for different reasons. Susy sings, "I can't afford to stand still." Ellie is always in motion, if she ever stopped, she'd realize the emptiness of her life. For this reason, make sure you keep the fizz in the champagne by staying conscious of the pace of the show. These are smart people who think quickly and say what they are thinking. Make sure the Susy and Nick story begins as a business transaction and grows surprisingly into a romance. Trust the humor, wit, and emotion of the show and play it honestly. Enjoy!

-Marc Bruni

SCENES AND MUSICAL NUMBERS

ACT ONE

Scene 1   The Vanderlyn Brownstone, Manhattan (April 1922)

"Living in the Modern Age" . . . . **COMPANY**

"The Proposal" . . . . **SUSY & NICK**

Scene 2   Streffy's Fishing Camp in Maine (June 1922)

"Cigars" . . . . **SUSY, STREFFY, NICK**

Scene 3   Ellie's Newport Mansion – Indoors and in the Garden (July-
              August 1922)

"Cigars" reprise . . . . **SUSY**

"Letters to Nelson" . . . . **ELLIE, NELSON**

"Glimpses of the Moon" . . . . **NICK, SUSY**

"The Glories of Greece" . . . . **CORAL, NICK**

"What Are You Waiting For?" . . . . **STREFFY, SUSY**

"Thank You for This" . . . . **ELLIE, SUSY**

"Dinner Party with Friends" . . . . **COMPANY**

"Can't You Hear That Jazz?" . . . . **SUSY, COMPANY**

ACT TWO

Scene 1   The Newport Regatta (August 1922 – the next day)

"Terrible News" . . . . **NELSON, STREFFY, COMPANY**

Scene 2   The bar of the Newport Yacht Club

"I'll Step Aside" . . . . **NICK, STREFFY**

Scene 3   The Barbizon Hotel – Manhattan (September 1922)

"Cigars" reprise . . . . **SUSY**

Scene 4   Bergdorf Goodman Fur Boutique, New York (the next day)

"That's What Money Can Buy" . . . . **CORAL, ELLIE**

Scene 5   Nick's Study/ Susy's Hotel, New York (several weeks later)

Scene 6   The Oak Room of the Algonquin Hotel, New York (October
              1922)

"Right Here, Right Now" . . . . **GUEST CABARET SINGER**

Scene 7   Outside Ellie's Brownstone (April 1923)

"Tell Her I'm Happy" . . . . **NELSON**

Scene 8   Inside Ellie's Brownstone / Outside The Hotel Nouveau Luxe

"But You're Not Him" . . . . **SUSY, NICK**

Scene 9   Outside the Hotel Nouveau Luxe

"Glimpses of the Moon" reprise . . . . **NICK, SUSY**

The writers wish to thank everyone who has been involved in the development and production of **GLIMPSES OF THE MOON**. We are grateful for the support and creative input of the cast, crew, producers and creative team, which together made this publication possible.

ACT ONE

Scene One

The Vanderlyn Brownstone An Anniversary Party
(April 1922)

(A jazz combo plays in the corner of the Vanderlyn's ball-room, set up for a party. **SUSY BRANCH** *dances into the empty room savoring the luxury, knowing at a glance the cost of each crystal vase and damask curtain. She is bright, pretty and practical, with a quick wit and natural grace that has helped her to remain popular, despite her lack of money. Susy gets by on invitations and small gifts from women like Ellie and Ursula, who depend on Susy to make their parties feel fun and modern.* **SUSY** *swipes a rose from an arrangement and considers the effect in her hair.)*

(Her friend **STREFFY** *– an English freeloader who dines out on Americans' fondness for royalty – enters and looks around appreciatively. Streffy is gossipy and selfish, but fun to have around. As the fourth in line for his family's title, he has no prospects, no career and no money, yet always manages to get by. He has long been secretly in love with Susy, but as he is too poor to marry anyone, has settled for being her friend and confidante.)*

STREFFY. Hello Susy dear!

SUSY. Streffy!

STREFFY. You look lovelier than the Vanderlyn's new Maxfield Parrish.

SUSY. I hear it cost buckets.

STREFFY. *(teasing, as he refills his private flask from a bottle on the bar)* Susy, it isn't nice to talk about money.

SUSY. *(lightly)* It's easy to not think about air as long as there's plenty to breathe.

9

STREFFY. Have you got enough to get by?

SUSY. Nope. But I'll think of something.

> (**ELLIE** and **NELSON VANDERLYN** enter. They are proper, upper-class, old-money Manhattan society. **ELLIE** is attractive, ambitious, generous when it suits her purposes, but otherwise completely self-centered and used to getting whatever she likes. Always competitive, she tries to keep up with rapidly changing times by playing jazz at her parties and learning the latest dances. **ELLIE** is always in motion; if she ever stopped, she'd realize the emptiness of her life. **NELSON** is a successful banker, a genial host, who wants the best for the wife he adores. **NELSON** presents her with an impressive necklace.)

NELSON. Happy Anniversary, Ellie Darling! These twenty years have been the happiest of my life.

ELLIE. (drooling over her new jewels) Oh Nelson! I do love your presents. So far 1922 has been a very good year. I can't wait to show Ursula.

SONG - LIVING IN THE MODERN AGE

(The doorbell chimes.)

> (**URSULA** – a vain society matron in a ridiculous hat – enters. She is even richer than **ELLIE**, her longtime rival.)

URSULA. Ellie!

ELLIE. Ursula!

GLAD TO SEE YOU DEAR!

URSULA.

LOVELY TO VISIT!

ELLIE.

LIKE THE PAINTING?

NELSON.

ONLY THE LATEST!

> (**SUSY & STREFFY** join the group.)

STREFFY.

ARE THEY PLAYING JAZZ?

URSULA & STREFFY.

AMBITIOUS!

ELLIE.

EVERYBODY'S HERE.

NELSON.

BA DE DE BA DE...

URSULA.

MARVELOUS PARTY!

ELLIE.

LET ME INTRODUCE YOU –

SUSY. *(to* **STREFFY***)*

GOD HOW I HATE THIS.

ALL.

HEAR THAT JAZZ!

STREFFY.

DELICIOUS!

URSULA. Ellie, how clever of you to build a ballroom in your own brownstone.

ELLIE. Ursula, meet Winthrop Strefford, next in line to be the Count of Altringham.

STREFFY. *(to* **SUSY***)* Fourth in line, but who's counting?

URSULA. Royalty! Well done! I'm bringing a scholar. Mr. Nick Lansing – from Harvard.

ELLIE. I've got the Count *and* I've asked Susy to dance, to keep the party...fun!

*(**NELSON** enters with champagne for everyone.)*

NELSON. A toast – to my lovely wife! To marriage!

(All raise their glasses in a toast.)

ALL.

LET THE PARTY START!

HEAR THE MUSIC PLAYING!

THE OLD WORLD MUST DEPART

MODERN WAYS ARE HERE TO STAY!

ALL. *(cont.)*

> CAN'T YOU UNDERSTAND?
> EVERYTHING'S IMPROVING
> EVERYTHING IS GRAND
> LOOK AT HOW WE LIVE TODAY!
>
> WE'RE DOING WELL
> WE'RE POS-O-LUTE-LY SWELL
> SURE, WEALTH IS A PLUS
> LIVING IN THIS MODERN AGE
>
> WE'VE GOT GIN JOINTS
> THE DOW HIT 90 POINTS
> YOU'D LIKE TO BE US
> LIVING IN THIS MODERN AGE.

NELSON. Streffy, join us in Newport this summer – come for the Regatta!

STREFFY. *(to* **SUSY***)* A fortnight of free meals!

SUSY. *(to* **STREFFY***)* I'd better wangle an invitation too. I'm nearly broke Streffy.

STREFFY. Don't worry my dear.

> *(He looks around and pockets the bread off the table.)*

I've been nearly broke my entire life.

> *(The doorbell chimes. Handsome archeologist* **NICK LANSING** *enters.)*

URSULA. This is my latest discovery: Mr. Nick Lansing. He's written a marvelous new book on Ancient Greek poetry –

NICK. Pottery, actually. Painted bowls, Grecian urns –

URSULA. – Terribly popular.

NICK. So far they've sold 27 copies.

STREFFY. *(to* **NICK***)* You're one of us– the underfed upper classes.

SUSY, STREFFY, NICK.

> WE'VE BEEN THROUGH DARK DAYS
> WE'LL HAVE BRIGHT TOMORROWS

NELSON.
> AND NOBODY PAYS
> ANY INCOME TAX SO FAR!

ELLIE, URSULA, NELSON.
> FOLLOW ALL THE FADS
> DRIVE AWAY YOUR SORROWS
> JUST LIKE IN THE ADS
> WHEN YOU BUY A PACKARD CAR.

ELLIE. *(taking* **SUSY** *aside)* Susy, your dress looks like last year's.

SUSY. It is. You gave it to me.

ELLIE. Be sure to dance with Nelson later. The old dear is rather fond of you.

> *(She hands* **SUSY** *a folded check, which* **SUSY** *reluctantly accepts and tucks away.)*

SUSY. You're terribly generous Ellie.

ELLIE. *(with genuine concern)* You can't live off your friends forever. As your father squandered your fortune before he died, your only chance is a suitable marriage. Hurry Susy! Marry anyone!

SUSY. Don't you believe in love?

ELLIE. I believe in Lehman Brothers.

SUSY. *(to herself)*
> IS THIS MY FATE?
> WASHED UP AT TWENTY-EIGHT?
> MY TIME'S RUNNING OUT....

SUSY. *(to* **NELSON**, *as she dances with him)* Mr. Vanderlyn, I wanted your advice...for a friend. How can she best invest her...capital?

NELSON. The market's up up up. How much has she got?

SUSY. *(opening the check)* Twenty?

NELSON. Thousand?

SUSY. Just Twenty.

NELSON. Ha!

> *(***NELSON** *breaks away to refill his glass.)*

SUSY. *(to herself)*

> A FRESHER FACE
> COULD QUICKLY TAKE MY PLACE

ELLIE, URSULA, NELSON, STREFFY.

> KEEP UP OR LOSE OUT!
> THAT'S WHAT IT'S ABOUT!
> LIVING IN THIS MODERN AGE

ELLIE. Susy, show us that new dance, the Lulu Wadu.

> *(**SUSY** dances the Lulu Wadu, an exuberant solo dance number.)*

ELLIE. Teach me a few steps.

SUSY. I don't think you'll like it.

ELLIE. I'll hate it, but one has to keep up. Popularity can be so precarious.

> *(**SUSY** demonstrates slowly. **ELLIE** imitates **SUSY**, awkwardly, and then finally gets the hang of it. **ELLIE** tries out her new moves with **NICK**. **URSULA** swoops in and snatches **NICK** away. Everyone joins in the big dance number. **NICK & SUSY** end up together – dancing impressively, while the others watch.)*

ALL.

> SHORTER FROCKS!
> HIGHER STOCKS!
> BARE YOUR KNEES!
> MODEL T'S!

SUSY. *(to **NICK**)* I'd better circulate. I promised Ellie I'd keep the party "fun."

NICK. Is that your racket?

SUSY. A man can make a fortune. A woman has to marry one.

NICK. And a man without a fortune?

STREFFY. Is unfortunate indeed.

ELLIE, NELSON, URSULA.

> SHORTER FROCKS AND HIGHER STOCKS IN THIS VERY
>   MODERN AGE

SUSY, NICK, STREFFY.

NOT A CENT TO PAY THE RENT IN THIS VERY MODERN AGE

ELLIE.

JEWELS ARE FINE, IF THEY ARE MINE.

NELSON.

LET'S GIVE THANKS FOR PRIVATE BANKS.

NICK.

BILLS TO PAY –

URSULA.

COME THIS WAY.

SUSY.

MUST BE WED.

STREFFY.

STEAL THE BREAD.

ALL.

AND OF COURSE, WE'VE GOT DIVORCE!

LIVING IN THE NOW
GOT TO HAVE THE LATEST
WE'LL GET BY SOMEHOW
MODERN TIMES ARE HERE TO STAY!

AINT WE GOT FUN!
SOMETHING FOR EVERYONE!
LATE NIGHT CABARETS –
BEING RICH REALLY PAYS
IN SO MANY WAYS!
LIVING IN THIS MODERN –

STREFFY & NICK.

THE COUNTRY'S DRY. CHAMPAGNE IS DRIER.
THE MARKET'S HIGH. WE'RE GETTING HIGHER

ALL.

– AGE!

WELCOME TO THIS MODERN AGE!

ELLIE. Everyone, we're playing charades in the drawing room!

(**NELSON** *and* **STREFFY** *exit.* **SUSY** *and* **NICK** *end up next to each other.*)

ELLIE. No sense leaving you two together, what a waste of clever conversation. Susy, you'll be on my team –

(**URSULA** *tries to pull* **NICK** *away in the other direction.*)

URSULA. Mr. Lansing will regale us with insights about Greek poetry.

NICK. Pottery!

URSULA. And I'll expect you to give a talk at my ladies' tea next week.

(**URSULA** *exits.*)

ELLIE. *(to* **SUSY***)* Say goodnight to the man and tell him there's no point seeing him again. He's poor.

(**ELLIE** *exits.*)

SUSY. Goodnight Mr. Lansing.

NICK. *(as* **SUSY** *starts to walk out)* Do you always do what Ellie tells you?

SUSY. Ellie does a lot for me. Her motor car will take me home from this party. I vacation with her every summer. So, I'd better go back.

(*She starts to leave again.*)

I'm very good at charades.

NICK. Don't you get tired of smiling on cue?

SUSY. Don't you get tired of being trotted out at parties, like a…box of chocolates?

NICK. I do real work. My trip to India with the Department Store Hickses, the Italian Art expedition with the Melroses. I was their resident historian and translator.

SUSY. Oh applesauce. Call it what you like. We take our fill of the art, culture, travel we need – in the only way we can…we're parasites.

NICK. The rich are worse. The Etruscan vases I discovered wound up as a birdbath in the Melrose gardens. I can't tolerate people taking things – no matter how ancient or beautiful – that do not belong to them.

SUSY. It seems to me you spend a good deal of your time among the social element you disapprove of.

NICK. I'd prefer not to be among society at all.

SUSY. Well, wet blanket, how else can you enjoy the advantages?

NICK. I wish I knew. Alexander the Great had conquered half of Asia by the age of 20. I'm still getting by writing entries for an encyclopedia of the ancient world. I'm up to D. Delphi, Delos, Dionysus. If I am ever to succeed, I have to find a way to write this year –

SUSY. I'm on a deadline too. My job is to marry – as soon as possible.

NICK. *(plowing ahead, not really listening to her)* – My novel would take place among the ruins I've studied – but it wouldn't be a history book – more of a philosophical treatise

SUSY. If you want it to sell, it should be romantic. An adventure, with castles and moonlight...

NICK. An adventure? Yes, I suppose it could be...But modern and challenging – like *Ulysses.*

SUSY. Joyce is a flat tire. Omitting punctuation doesn't make a book modern – just hard to read.

URSULA. *(offstage)* Mr. Lansing!

ELLIE. *(offstage)* Susy!

SUSY. Back to work. It isn't that simple to find the right person. I'm terribly poor and have very expensive tastes.

NICK. You'd want those splifficated swells in Ellie's drawing room?

SUSY. I can't let Ellie's prime list go to waste. You can only meet the right sort of people at the right dinners and trips and country house weekends. I don't know how many more chances I'll have – to find someone.

NICK. But you're popular, the live wire of every party.

SUSY. I've seen what happens to unmarried girls if they don't have their own fortune. They're reduced to running errands or being a companion for someone's aunt... Married couples get invited everywhere – and I'd meet so many new people...

NICK. So you need a husband...in order to secure a better one?

(Music begins as the plan forms in SUSY's mind.)

SUSY. Now that's the ticket!

NICK. *(starting to walk away)* You'll handcuff some flush fellow. Ellie will throw you a party in her ballroom, you'll be showered with presents.

SUSY. The rich do love buying gifts. By getting married, I'd almost be doing them a favor....

SONG - THE PROPOSAL

SUSY.	NICK.
I WAS THINKING	
	WHAT?
YOU'LL SAY I'M CRAZY –	
	NO.
ABOUT A WEDDING BASH.	
	Why?
THINK OF THE PARTIES.	
	YES?
THINK OF THE PRESENTS	
	SO?
AND THINK OF ALL THAT CASH!	
	But what has that got to do with us?

SUSY.
WE'LL MARRY, NOT FOR LOVE, BUT FOR MONEY.
NICK.
BUT DARLING, YOU KNOW I DON'T HAVE A DIME.
SUSY.
WE'LL MARRY, NOT FOR LOVE, BUT FOR MONEY.

NICK.

MONEY?

SUSY.

YES FOR MONEY.

TILL WE FIND LOVE, WE'LL HAVE A LOVELY TIME.

We're both unusually popular

We're sure to get heaps of gifts!

NICK. Let me get this straight –

WE'LL MARRY, NOT FOR LOVE, BUT FOR MONEY?

How will we get it?

SUSY.

WE'LL TRADE IN EVERY SILVER TABLESPOON.

WE BOTH HAVE WEALTHY FRIENDS WHO'LL GIVE DINNERS, LINENS,

BRAND NEW LUGGAGE

AND SEND US ON A YEAR-LONG HONEY MOON.

While we live off the gifts, you can write your novel.

We'll have plenty of time to find appropriate partners.

I HATE BEING DEPENDENT ON OUR FRIENDS' GOOD GRACES

NICK.

ALWAYS SMILING HARD.

SUSY.

PUTTING ON YOUR NICEST FACES

SUSY & NICK.

NEVER LETTING DOWN YOUR GUARD

NICK.

IF WE PURSUED THIS SCHEME AS SPOUSES

WE COULD GET AWAY

SUSY.

WE COULD HAVE OUR PICK OF HOUSES

HERE'S MY PROPOSAL, WHAT DO YOU SAY?

NICK.

WE'LL MARRY AND WE'LL SAIL,

SUSY & NICK.

    SOMEWHERE SUNNY!

    TOGETHER WE'LL BE FREE OF ALL OUR CARES

    WE'LL MARRY NOT FOR LONG, BUT FOR MONEY

SUSY.

    MONEY!

NICK.

    YES, MY HONEY

SUSY.

    WE'LL HELP EACH OTHER MARRY MILLIONAIRES

    *(**SUSY** and **NICK** run off while the others enter as wedding guests with gifts, checks and invitations to their houses. **SUSY** returns wearing a veil, with a bridal bouquet. **NICK** sports a top hat. During the music, they have a wedding and dance down the aisle.)*

STREFFY. Congratulations!

URSULA. Do come to Kent – for the foliage!

NELSON. And don't forget Newport!

ELLIE. Yes! July would be perfect.

STREFFY. You must begin your honeymoon at my fishing camp in Maine.

    *(**SUSY** tosses her bouquet. **ELLIE** fights off **URSULA** and catches it. The guests all exit.)*

NICK.

    WHEN YOU FIND SOMEONE ELSE WHO HAS MONEY –

SUSY. Perhaps a baron?

NICK. Maybe an heiress?

SUSY & NICK.

    I PROMISE TO RELINQUISH YOU OF COURSE

    WE'LL NEVER QUARREL, NEVER FIGHT

    I WON'T ASK WHERE YOU WERE LAST NIGHT

    WE'LL SIMPLY SAY GOODBYE WITHOUT REMORSE

    AND IN A YEAR, WE'LL HAVE A SWEET DIVORCE.

    (blackout)

Scene Two
Streffy's Fishing Camp In Maine

(June 1922)

*(**NICK** and **SUSY** have married and spent a month in Streffy's rustic cottage.)*

*(On their last day, while **SUSY** packs and takes inventory, **NICK** slaps at mosquitoes.)*

SUSY. It was very decent of you to sleep outside on the porch for the whole month. Streffy's cousins have dreary castles in Scotland. All he has is this cottage – in Maine.

NICK. It's a fishing shack!

SUSY. With roses and seashells...

NICK. And mosquitoes.

SUSY. At any rate, we're leaving today. New renters arrive tomorrow –

NICK. I'm surprised you chose this place. No parties, not a millionaire for miles.

SUSY. I planned our visits so we'd arrive at Ellie's place in Newport at the height of the Season. And I thought you'd get a lot of writing done here – no distractions.

NICK. No inspiration. What's left of our collection of wedding gifts?

SUSY. *(checking her calendar and calculations)* Well, in the last four weeks, we've sold off the entire dinner service and the crystal. If we're careful and creative, we ought to be able to make it last a year –

NICK. A year of freedom.

SUSY. No keeping Ellie company at the dressmaker!

NICK. No Ursulas insisting I talk at her teas.

SUSY. No troubles, no deadlines...

NICK. *(taking a cigar from the box and sniffing it)* And these excellent cigars! How did Streffy get so many? A case of Havanas costs a fortune.

SUSY. Someone must have forgotten them here.

NICK. How are we getting to Newport? The train tickets are awfully expensive. The Baccarat lighter?

SUSY. That's for October.

(She opens the trunk to see if any items were overlooked.)

All our gifts are already accounted for – or sent on ahead.

NICK. So we have no money and no way to get to Newport? You told me you had this all planned out?

SUSY. *(suddenly realizing that she miscalculated)* I do. I mean – I will. I just need to think –

NICK. When I was travelling in India with the Hickses, if we missed the train, they'd have a chauffeured car waiting

SUSY. *(thinking quickly)* That's it! The maid's beau is a chauffeur, who has to be in Newport for another job tomorrow. I'm sure he'd take us, if I could just find him something as a thank you tip.

(SUSY looks around, picks up a decorative plate, polishes it, considers it as a gift.)

NICK. That's not one of ours, its Streffy's.

SUSY. But he hates it. It was a gift from Ellie and he's always threatening to smash it.

NICK. You can't take other people's things. I'd sooner walk to Newport.

SUSY. I'll manage something. Go, I'll finish packing.

(NICK exits. SUSY starts to pack up the wedding presents. As she puts them in the trunk, she calculates their worth.)

SONG - CIGARS

SUSY. *(cont.)*

(spoken) Silver candlesticks…two meals out
Crystal flower vase…pay the cook

(She reaches for the box of **STREFFY**'s *cigars – but hesitates.)*

SHOULD I TAKE THE CIGARS?
WELL, HE SAID THEY WERE OURS,
TO ENJOY IN HIS PLACE.
BUT TO TAKE THE WHOLE CASE
SEEMS A LITTLE TOO FAR.
STILL, IT'S JUST A CIGAR.

(She leaves the cigars and resumes her packing.)

(spoken) Gold rimmed teacups…the butcher's bill
Set of lobster forks…the cleaners fee…

(In her imagination, Streffy joins the debate. **STREFFY**
appears in a red light amid wafting bubbles.)

STREFFY.

GO ON, TAKE THE CIGARS!
EMPTY OUT THE ARMOIRS!
I LEFT THEM AROUND
JUST LIKE CASH ON THE GROUND
THEY WERE MEANT TO BE FOUND.
YOU DRANK GIN FROM MY BAR
WHY NOT TAKE THE CIGAR?

(Amid more bubbles, imaginary **NICK** *appears in white.)*

NICK.

DON'T YOU TAKE THE CIGARS!
CAN'T YOU SEE HOW IT MARS
BOTH MY ROSY WORLD VIEW
AND WHAT I THINK OF YOU?
IS YOUR PRIZE WORTH THE SCAR?
IF YOU TAKE THE CIGAR?

*(***STREFFY*** and* **NICK** *hover over* **SUSY** *like the devil/
angel of her conscience.)*

SUSY.	STREFFY.	NICK.
	WHILE YOU SIT AROUND DEBATING, RIGHT OUTSIDE, THE CHAUFFEUR'S WAITING.	
JUST DECIDE OR I'LL LOSE ALL I HAVE ARRANGED.		
		WHAT YOU'RE CONTEMPLATING'S AWFUL –
AND PERHAPS A BIT UNLAWFUL		
		DARLING, IN THIS MONTH, BOTH YOU AND I HAVE CHANGED.
	OH JUST IGNORE HIM.	
SHOULD I TAKE THE CIGARS?- –		
		IF YOU DO THIS YOU'LL REGRET IT.
	ONLY IF YOU LET IT.	
		I'M AFRAID YOU MIGHT BECOME SOMEONE I'D HATE.
SOMEONE I WOULD HATE SHOULD I TAKE THE CIGARS?		
	MUST YOU HAVE SUCH UPTIGHT MORALS?	
		MUST YOU MIX IN OTHERS' QUARRELS?

STREFFY & NICK.

> WHILE YOU'RE AT IT, TAKE THE SOAP,
> IT'S NOT TOO LATE.

> *(quickly, overlapping)*

NICK. How could you?!

STREFFY. How could you not?

SUSY. I don't even smoke!

NICK. What does this mean?

STREFFY. Sometimes a cigar is just a cigar.

SUSY.	**STREFFY.**	**NICK.**
SHOULD I TAKE –		
	YOU SHOULD TAKE –	
		NO, DON'T TAKE –
THE CIGARS!	THE CIGARS!	THE CIGARS! DON'T TAKE THE CIGARS!
SHOULD I SEE THIS THING THROUGH?		
	GO ON! SEE THIS THROUGH –	

> *(**NICK** and **STREFFY** exit)*

SUSY.

> I'M NO COMMON THIEF
> AND IT'S MY TRUE BELIEF
> AND I KNOW HE'D AGREE –
> IF IT BUYS ONE MORE WEEK
> OF BEING TRULY FREE.

> *(**SUSY** packs the case of cigars and shuts the trunk.)*

> *(blackout)*

Scene 3
Ellie Vanderlyn's Newport Mansion
(July 1922)

(A MAID enters and illuminates the many rooms. A grand chandelier descends. NICK and SUSY enter and take in their new opulent surroundings. While NICK runs back and forth exploring, the maid takes SUSY's suitcase.)

MAID. Welcome to Vanderhaven. I'll unpack your things, Mrs. Lansing.

SUSY. Mrs. Lansing?

MAID. The gardener asked you to approve the flowers for the hall arrangements. Cook is waiting to review the menus. And the butler wants to know what you'd like from the bootlegger.

SUSY. *(calling)* Ellie!

MAID. *(handing her a pink note from ELLIE)* Mrs. Vanderlyn left a note for you, Mrs. Lansing.

SUSY. Isn't she here?

MAID. No.

SUSY. But where –

MAID. Didn't say where, didn't say when she'll be back.

(The MAID exits with the suitcase. SUSY opens the letter. ELLIE appears in a spotlight, holding a fan of sealed envelopes.)

ELLIE. Dear Susy – I do hope you like my humble cottage. You and Nick are welcome to stay all summer. Just a tiny favor, be an angel and post these letters to Nelson each week. So he'll think I'm here with you. There's no need for Nelson to know where I've gone, or with whom. I've numbered the letters so you'll know when to send them. I'm sure I can count on you to erase the numbers and mail them yourself. *(She places the letters on a table.)* Gratefully yours, Ellie.

(ELLIE exits. SUSY sings a reprise of CIGARS.)

SUSY.

> IT'S ANOTHER CIGAR –
> MORE AMORAL BY FAR
> IF I DO AS SHE ASKS
> WILL THESE TERRIBLE TASKS
> DEFINE WHO WE ARE?
>
> A FEW LETTERS TO SEND.
> ONE SMALL LIE FOR A FRIEND.
> THE HOUSE IS SO NICE...
> IS IT TOO HIGH A PRICE?
> SHOULD WE JUST LEAVE TODAY?

> *(SUSY considers the letter in her hand. NICK bursts in.)*

NICK. Susy, look at the view from my study! I can't wait to write my novel here. Thank you, my brilliant resourceful Susy, for all this! Where's Ellie?

SUSY. Oh. She's away...

NICK. That's odd. Where did she go?

SUSY. *(making it up)* She's at...a cure.

NICK. So this is all ours...I claim the entire North wing!

> *(NICK runs off.)*

SUSY.

> I GUESS THIS MEANS WE'LL STAY.

> *(The MAID enters, hands SUSY her purse and a pencil. SUSY erases the number on Letter #1. The maid exits.)*

SUSY. *(calling to NICK)* Nick, I'm off to the Post Office. I brought the Social Register. I'm going to meet all the neighbors.

> *(SUSY takes the letter and exits. ELLIE appears singing LETTERS TO NELSON #1.)*

> *(During the course of the seven weeks covered by this song, SUSY and NICK's relationship slowly evolves from a business deal to friendship and finally to love.)*

> *(Meanwhile, ELLIE narrates her letters from afar, appearing in various outfits of seductive undress, as she cavorts with her unseen lover.)*

ELLIE. Newport, July Tenth.
> NELSON, MY DARLING.
> I MISS YOU – A LOT.
> YESTERDAY IT RAINED,
> TODAY IT DID NOT.
>
> OUR DAYS ARE SO DULL HERE
> THE COOK HAS THE FLU
> I'M SITTING HERE SULKING
> AND THINKING OF YOU.

> *(***ELLIE*** exits.)*

> *(One week later –* **SUSY** *and* **NICK** *bump into each other from opposite ends of the enormous mansion.)*

NICK. Susy! I haven't seen you all week.

SUSY. Being married has definitely improved my popularity. I've been busy with a bachelor from the Breakers.

NICK. Does your boyfriend mind that you're married?

SUSY. Married simply means not yet divorced.

NICK. Isn't he awfully old?

SUSY. Ancient. How's the book?

> *(The* **MAID** *enters, hands* **SUSY** *a wrapped wedding gift box and exits.)*

NICK. Still working on a title.

SUSY. I'm off to the pawn shop and the post office. Say goodbye to the "footed compote."

> *(***SUSY*** exits with gift box.)*

NICK. Bye!

> *(Lights down on* **NICK,** *staring at his typewriter.)*

> *(In a spotlight,* **ELLIE** *sings* ***LETTERS TO NELSON #2.****)*

ELLIE. Newport, July 21st.
> NELSON MY DARLING
> HOW'S WORK AT THE BANK?
> I FIRED THE BUTLER
> THEY SAY THAT HE DRANK.

ELLIE. *(cont.)*

    I'M WATCHING THE SUNSET
    WITH NOTHING TO DO
    I'M DUSTING YOUR PICTURE
    AND THINKING OF YOU.

    *(***ELLIE*** exits.)*

    (Two weeks later. **NICK** *is seated at his typewriter, not writing much.* **SUSY** *enters and joins him at his desk.)*

SUSY. I've been invited to the Berwind Ball at the Elms! I bought you a new ribbon for your typewriter.

    *(***SUSY*** *hands* **NICK** *the typewriter ribbon and then opens an envelope from Arthur Murray's mail order dance school.)*

NICK. I wish I needed it. I'm having trouble establishing my protagonist...

SUSY. *(placing the numbered footprints on the floor)* Start off right in the middle of something exciting –

NICK. That's what Aristotle suggests.

    (suddenly noticing **SUSY** *following the footprints on the floor)*

    What are you doing?

SUSY. I can Lulu or Lame Duck with my eyes shut. But – on the level – I never learned how to waltz. I can't make a fool of myself at the Berwind Ball.

    *(***SUSY*** *tries to follow the diagrams on the floor, but gets it all wrong.)*

NICK. You're making a mess of things. Here.

    *(***NICK*** *picks up the footprints. He positions* **SUSY**'s *arms, corrects the tilt of her chin. She looks at her feet. He lifts her chin, laughs at her in a brotherly way. They dance together, slowly at first. They continue while* **ELLIE** *sings **LETTER TO NELSON #3**.)*

ELLIE. Newport August 7th

    NELSON MY DARLING
    THE LANSINGS ARE HERE...

ELLIE. *(cont.)*

> SHE'S KEEPING THINGS LIVELY
> HE'S RATHER SINCERE
>
> I'M AWFULLY GLAD
> THAT WE ASKED THEM TO STAY.
> THEIR LOVE IS SO NEW,
> THEY EMBRACE EACH NEW DAY.
> CAN YOU REMEMBER WHEN WE WERE THAT WAY?

*(As the music swells, **NICK** and **SUSY**'s dancing becomes more fluid and more romantic.)*

> NELSON, MY DARLING....

*(Lights fade on **ELLIE**.)*

*(Two weeks later, **NICK** paces near his desk, while **SUSY** finishes his latest chapter.)*

NICK. Well?

SUSY. It's wonderful, Nick. You've made such progress over the last few weeks. I love the way the story starts with the chariot race winner realizing that his wheel is broken.

NICK. Did you understand that the narrator is the artist, painting the scene on a clay bowl –

SUSY. – So the thrill of that day will always be remembered. Yes! You're a good writer Nick.

NICK. I found my inspiration.

SUSY. I met someone interesting this afternoon.

*(**SUSY** hands **NICK** the business card.)*

NICK. Knopf? The publisher? Are you going out with him again?

SUSY. No, silly! He's expecting your novel.

NICK. I'd better finish it!

*(**NICK** starts to type furiously as **SUSY** exits with the letter.)*

*(**ELLIE**, wearing only a rumpled bedsheet, sings **LETTER TO NELSON #4**.)*

ELLIE.

ALGIE MY DARLING. Ahem.

(**NELSON** *appears in spotlight, reading the letter.*)

ELLIE.	**NELSON.**
NELSON MY DARLING,	
WHAT MORE CAN I SAY?	WHAT MORE CAN I SAY?
SO LITTLE GOES ON	
WHILE YOU ARE AWAY	WHILE YOU ARE AWAY
I'M REDECORATING	
– A MUCH BRIGHTER HUE	A MUCH BRIGHTER HUE
I'M SPENDING YOUR MONEY	SHE'S SPENDING MY MONEY
AND THINKING OF	AND THINKING OF –
NELSON MY DARLING!	– ME!

(*Lights out on* **ELLIE** *and* **NELSON**.)

(**NICK** *pulls a last page out of the typewriter, as* **SUSY** *enters.*)

NICK. Susy! I've finished the first section of "Love Among the Ruins." Will you tell me if it's any good?

SUSY. Of course I'll read it. Tonight! I'm so proud of you Nick, so pleased for you.

NICK. I love being here with you – being truly free. Look, there's our moon already rising!

(*They stroll together in the moonlight.*)

SUSY. People with a balance in the bank can't be as happy as this.

NICK. I detest people with a balance. Though I do like their houses. Fortunately the view is ours, free of charge.

SUSY. Well, until Ellie comes back – it could be as soon as tomorrow.

NICK. Let her come, it won't change anything between us.

SUSY. Won't it?

NICK. Being married changes a person. It's as if we belong to each other. I've never had something that I really wanted. That wasn't handed down like a faded evening cloak or a borrowed motorcar. But now I do!

SUSY. Yes! Being here with you – in this glorious place – with our own gardener and butler and all these rooms –

NICK. Is that all this summer has meant to you? Servants and gilded houses?

SUSY. No, of course not!

NICK. But you should have them…

SONG - GLIMPSES OF THE MOON

NICK. *(cont.)*

I WISH I COULD GIVE YOU MORE
THAN MOONBEAMS ON THE SEA
I CAN ONLY GIVE YOU SUNSETS
AND READ YOU POETRY

THINGS YOU PROB'LY WOULDN'T MISS
I WISH I COULD GIVE YOU SOMETHING
MORE THAN THIS.

SUSY.

I WISH I COULD GIVE YOU MORE
REAL TREASURES MADE OF GOLD
SOMETHING RARE YOU'VE DREAMED OF FINDING
TOO PRECIOUS TO BE SOLD

MAKE A WISH ON ALL THE STARS
THAT THIS BORROWED WORLD
MIGHT SOMEDAY ALL BE OURS.

NICK & SUSY.

THROW THE CALENDAR AWAY
I CAN'T BEAR TO BREAK THE SPELL.
WHEN THE NIGHT FADES INTO DAY
AND WE HAVE TO LEAVE AS WELL.

WE'LL BUILD CASTLES IN THE AIR –
IN THIS YEAR WE HAVE TOGETHER
WE'VE TIME TO DREAM AND DARE

NICK & SUSY. *(cont.)*

CLOUDS WILL FILL THE SKY TOO SOON.
I CAN ONLY GIVE YOU
GLIMPSES OF THE MOON.

(For the very first time, they kiss.)

STREFFY. *(as he enters and interrupts)* Ahoy, honeymooners! What's for dinner?

SUSY. Streffy!

STREFFY. I figured you'd be tired of your business proposition by now and ready for gossip and serious conversation.

NICK. I was looking forward to a quiet evening with my wife.

STREFFY. When two people are as popular as you and Susy, you can't expect privacy. Yachts are lining up to get a look at you. The financial houses are taking bets on how long you can make it last.

NICK. Indefinitely darling, would you say? *(He kisses **SUSY**.)* See you at dinner.

*(**NICK** exits.)*

STREFFY. Where's Nick going?

SUSY. He's writing.

STREFFY. Rot, what's he writing?

SUSY. He works on his novel for hours every day.

STREFFY. He's breaking you in dear, establishing an alibi. Let's follow him.

SUSY. Nick and I don't need alibis. We promised to release each other if either of us finds a chance to marry wealthily.

STREFFY. Capital. But how can you be sure that when Nick wants a change, that you'll agree?

SUSY. If he no longer wants to be with me, I hope I shall have enough common sense to leave him.

STREFFY. Love and common sense never go together. If I were in love with someone, I'd never leave her side, even if she married someone else. Even if the idea of loving me never crossed her pretty head. Of course, I can't afford to even contemplate the possibility of marriage.

SUSY. If your relatives died and you inherited the fortune, you'd marry tomorrow, you know you would.

STREFFY. The Lords of Altringham are known for their longevity. All that sportsmanship. I'll never have the title. However I received an outrageous rental fee on my fishing camp. They took it for seven weeks!

SUSY. Who are they anyway?

STREFFY. Oh –

(An awkward pause – **STREFFY** *looks away.)*

SUSY. Your renters?

STREFFY. A pair of love sick idiots.

(changing the subject)

Guess whose yacht just arrived in town? Those dreadful department store Hickses.

(Lights fade on **SUSY** *and* **STREFFY** *in the garden.)*

(Meanwhile, **NICK** *is reviewing his manuscript.)*

*(***CORAL HICKS*** arrives. She is a sturdy, socially awkward intellectual wearing thick glasses and a safari suit.)*

CORAL. *(calling from offstage)* Yoo hoo! Is anyone home?

*(***CORAL*** *enters. She sneaks up on* **NICK.***)*

Guess who?? It's me, Coral Hicks! Don't you recognize me, Mr. Lansing? From my family's trip to India? You were the best resident historian we ever had. I majored in Ancient History at Bryn Mawr, because of you. While I was sitting in class, memorizing the dates of the Peloponnesian battles, I was always thinking of... you.

NICK. Coral, you're all grown up.

CORAL. I never was young, if that's what you mean. It's lucky my parents gave me such a grand education. For my graduate thesis, I'm studying the role of women in ancient religions – an area where they had actual power and influence. And Daddy agreed we could all go in the yacht and tour the Greek islands for my research on the priestesses of the Eleusinian mysteries. Will you join us?

NICK. It is a dreadful temptation.

CORAL. We had a grand time in India together. Greece will be even better.

NICK. Everything's different now.

CORAL. Mr. Buttles – our resident historian and translator – has left the cruise – for personal reasons. And I asked Daddy if you could come along instead.

NICK. I'm sticking to my writing.

CORAL. Oh. But what about your real work – your research into kalyxes and kraters?

NICK. Archeology doesn't pay. I'm counting on my novel to be a success. It's the only way I can think of that Susy and I could possibly stay together.

CORAL. But your novel may fail.

NICK. If you stopped to consider such things, no one would write – or take any sort of chance.

CORAL. I brought you a present.

(She hands him a large painted potshard from her field bag.)

NICK. A fifth century Euphronius fragment! It's beautiful. Where's the rest of the pot?

CORAL. In Naxos. Daddy bought this one from Lord Elgin's collection. But there's more…waiting, to be… unearthed. Read the inscription.

NICK. *(He starts to read the inscription – in Greek.)*
Hóti mèn humeîs, hô ándres Athēnaîoi,

SONG - THE GLORIES OF GREECE

CORAL.   NICK.

SPEAK TO ME,   *Pepónthate hupò tôn emôn*
                                          katēgórōn, ouk oîda: eg d'
                                          oûn kaì autòs hup'

IN GREEK TO ME
STAY WITH ME A WHILE
SEE WONDERS OF THE
WORLD
ON AN ANCIENT ISLE

(Noticing **NICK** *has stopped reading, she turns over the shard. He continues reading as she sings.)*

                                          hautōn olígou emautoû
                                          epelathómēn.

THE MYSTERY OF HISTORY
THE MARVEL OF IT ALL
ESCAPE THE HOI POLLOI
HEED THE SIRENS' CALL!

DEAD LANGUAGES THRILL ME
AND HEROES FROM DAYS OF YORE
TELL ME MORE!
LET'S EXPLORE!
ALL THE GLOR-IES OF GREECE.

(Lights fade on **NICK & CORAL**. *Lights up on* **SUSY & STREFFY** *in the garden.)*

STREFFY. You'd better watch out for Coral. That girl's education won't stand in her way. Nick may have found his patron of the arts. You ought to look around Susy. Perhaps a prince at the International Ball this evening.

SUSY. Oh I can't, I promised Nick I'd read his manuscript.

*(***STREFFY*** holds out the invitation tempting* **SUSY** *with it.)*

STREFFY. You'd pass up the most elegant event of the year, a chance to meet dozens of wealthy and interesting royals, to sit home and read Nick's scribblings? Your priorities are out of order, my dear. You can't live forever off pawned cutlery.

SONG - WHAT ARE YOU WAITING FOR?

STREFFY. *(cont.)*

> THERE'S A WORLD OUTSIDE YOUR WINDOW
> THERE'S A CHANCE YOU CAN'T IGNORE.
> FIND THE FORTUNE YOU'VE BEEN SEEKING!
> WHAT ARE YOU WAITING FOR?

> TAKE A LOOK OUTSIDE YOUR WINDOW
> THERE'S A DANCE OUTSIDE YOUR DOOR
> BE THE PRINCESS AT THE BALL!
> WHAT ARE YOU WAITING FOR?

> AS FRIENDS I FEEL IT'S MY DUTY
> TO MAKE THE MOST OF YOUR BEAUTY
> OFF WE GO,
> DON'T SAY NO
> YOU SHOULD HAVE SO MUCH MORE
> SO, WHAT ARE YOU WAITING FOR?

(Lights up on both scenes.)

CORAL.

> WHAT AN OPPORTUNITY
> TO VOYAGE ON THE WINE DARK SEA.
> LIKE PLATO AND DEMOSTHENES
> DEBATE THE GREAT DEMOCRACIES

STREFFY.

> FORGET THE SWEET ROMANTIC THRILLS
> YOU NEED A PRINCE TO PAY YOUR BILLS

CORAL/STREFFY.

> LIKE SPARTANS AT THERMOPOLAE
> I WON'T GIVE UP UNTIL I DIE~

*(**STREFFY**'s verses repeat in counterpoint to **CORAL**'s.)*

CORAL.	**STREFFY.**
SPEAK TO ME,	THERE'S A WORLD OUTSIDE YOUR WINDOW
IN GREEK TO ME	THERE'S A CHANCE YOU CAN'T IGNORE
STAY WITH ME A WHILE	FIND THE FORTUNE YOU'VE BEEN SEEKING

CORAL.	STREFFY.
SEE WONDERS OF THE WORLD ON AN ANCIENT ISLE	
	WHAT ARE YOU WAITING FOR?

CORAL & NICK.	STREFFY & SUSY.
THE MYSTERY OF HISTORY	TAKE A LOOK OUTSIDE YOUR WINDOW
THE MARVEL OF IT ALL	THERE'S A DANCE OUTSIDE YOUR DOOR
ESCAPE THE HOI POLLOI	BE THE PRINCESS AT THE BALL!
HEED THE SIRENS' CALL	WHAT ARE YOU WAITING FOR?

NICK.	SUSY.
DEAD LANGUAGES THRILL ME	ONE GLANCE AND THEY'LL ALL BE STARING

CORAL.	STREFFY.
AND HEROES FROM DAYS OF YORE	LET'S SEE WHAT EVERYONE'S WEARING

CORAL.	NICK	STREFFY & SUSY.
TELL ME MORE	ESCAPE THE HOI POLLOI	OFF WE GO,
LET'S EXPLORE	WE'LL FIND ANOTHER TROY	DON'T SAY NO.
ALL THE GLORIES	ON THE AEGEAN SHORE	THERE'S A WORLD TO
OF GREECE		EXPLORE

STREFFY, CORAL, SUSY, NICK.
SO WHAT ARE YOU –
WHAT ARE YOU –
WHAT ARE YOU
WAITING –
FOR?

CORAL. I'll go cable Daddy that you're joining us!

NICK. Wait, I need to think about this.

CORAL. He'll be so excited!

(squawk of a car horn)

CORAL. Did you hear a motorcar?

*(**CORAL** exits.)*

(squawk!)

STREFFY. Sounds like your lease is up.

SUSY.	**NICK.**
I've got to find Nick!	Susy!

*(**NICK** exits.)*

STREFFY. *(to **SUSY**)* Where will you go next? To the Ball!

*(**ELLIE** enters carrying a travelling case.)*

ELLIE. Hello darlings, I'm back. I had the most wonderful time. Hello Streffy! Come Susy, help me with my things.

SUSY. *(to **STREFFY**)* Tell the cook to prepare another place.

*(**STREFFY** exits with **ELLIE**'s coat and case.)*

SUSY. Ellie! Where have you been?

ELLIE. Oh Susy, it was so perfect! I was meant to be happy.

SUSY. Weren't we all?

ELLIE. Oh no dearest. Not housekeepers and mothers-in-law and nannies. They wouldn't know happiness if they fell over it. But you and I darling…we deserve it.

SUSY. How could you put me in this awkward position!

ELLIE. I can't imagine it was so very difficult. Did the servants give you any trouble?

SUSY. No, it was all lovely. But now that you're back – the lying is over.

ELLIE. Of course, if you happen to see Nelson, I'll expect you to tell him what a wonderful summer we all had here – together.

SUSY. I won't lie to poor old Nelson.

ELLIE. But you must!

SONG - THANK YOU FOR THIS

ELLIE.

WHEN YOU CAME TO STAY
YOU LET ME GO AWAY
A SUMMER OF SECRET HAPPINESS
AN ISLAND ALONE
WHERE MY LIFE WAS MY OWN

FOR BAREFOOT WALKS, QUIET TALKS – WE WENT FISHING.
FOR LETTING ME LIVE THE WAY YOU DO.

FOR EACH PERFECT NIGHT!
FOR EACH PERFECT DAY!
THANK YOU.

I have a little gift for you.

(**ELLIE** gives **SUSY** a jeweled bracelet.)

SUSY. Oh Ellie! Thank you.

FOR TENNIS GAMES, MARBLE HALLS, ALL THESE SERVANTS.

SUSY & ELLIE.

FOR LETTING ME LIVE –
THE WAY YOU DO.

FOR ALL THAT WE SHARED.
FOR ALL THAT WE DARED.
THANK YOU FOR THIS.

WOMEN LIKE US CAN'T RAISE OUR VOICES
CAN'T DEFY SOCIAL PREJUDICE
HAVING YOUR FRIENDSHIP GAVE ME CHOICES…

ELLIE.	**SUSY.**
	THIS! –
BAREFOOT WALKS, QUIET TALKS,	
SIMPLE PLEASURES	
THANK YOU –	THANK YOU FOR
	TENNIS GAMES,
	MARBLE HALLS
	ALL THIS FREEDOM

BOTH.

FOR TIME ALONE, SPENT ON MY OWN, A DREAM COME TRUE

THANK YOU!	THANK YOU!

ELLIE. Now, I must get my wardrobe together, and then I'm off for Southampton. I asked Nelson to bring some of my clothes from New York, but I want to clear out before he arrives. So, you'll send them on –

SUSY. Nelson is coming – here?

ELLIE. Don't worry, he isn't due 'til tomorrow. I'll be off before dull old Nelson arrives.

*(***NELSON*** pounces into the room.)*

NELSON. Caught you at it!

ELLIE. Hello darling! You wonderful, wonderful man! Did you bring my clothes? I do have to catch the train to South Hampton.

NELSON. Let's have a delightful supper together before you go.

SUSY. She has to catch a train –

NELSON. So do I. We can take the late train together. I'll tell Cook to set another place.

*(***NELSON*** exits.)*

SUSY. What will we say??

ELLIE. I rely on you to figure it out. You're always so… resourceful.

*(***NICK*** enters.)*

NICK. Ellie! So glad you're back!

ELLIE. You won't say anything –

NICK. About what?

*(***SUSY*** interrupts and tries to keep them apart.)*

SUSY. About your novel. Ellie is exhausted from her trip, but she wants to hear all about it.

*(***SUSY*** pushes **ELLIE** towards the door.)*

So, you keep working on your book, and we'll all catch up at dinner.

*(***CORAL*** bounces into the room.)*

CORAL. *(to* **NICK***)* I cabled Daddy and they've arranged everything –

NICK. *(to* CORAL*)* Shh!

(to others)

She's arranged –uh – to stay for dinner. *(introducing her)* Coral Hicks. I'll tell Cook to set another –

(STREFFY *enters.)*

STREFFY. Did someone mention dinner? Count me in.

NICK. Two more places.

(ELLIE *exits.* NICK *and* CORAL *exit.* SUSY *pulls* STREFFY *aside.)*

SUSY. Streffy, I need your help here. Can you keep a secret? about Ellie – and Nelson.

STREFFY. Lord! That's hardly a secret. Everyone knows about Ellie's adventures, except Nelson, of course.

SUSY. I'm worried someone might say something.

STREFFY. You won't, I won't, Nick –

SUSY. Nick doesn't even suspect. And if he should find out that I knew, that we owed this summer to my knowing….

STREFFY. Good Lord, doesn't he know that you know?

SUSY. If he knew that I knew, what we know –

STREFFY. Does Ellie know that Nick doesn't know what we know?

SUSY. I don't know.

STREFFY. Jove.

(As STREFFY *takes* SUSY*'s hand,* NELSON *comes upon them.)*

NELSON. Well, well, so I've caught you at it! Susy! Streffy!

(STREFFY *laughs uncomfortably.)*

STREFFY. Hullo Old Nelson, how goes the banking world at Vanderlyn & Co?

(ELLIE, NICK *and* CORAL *enter, ready for dinner.)*

NELSON. Tell me what's been going on in my house? Ellie, I received your letters – I see the butler is back.

ELLIE. Back? Where did he go?

NELSON. *(affectionately)* The one you fired. Isn't that what you wrote in your letter? Weren't you here running this house all summer?

SONG - DINNER PARTY WITH FRIENDS

SUSY.

Ah ah – AREN'T YOU TIRED FROM ALL YOUR TRAVELS?

DON'T YOU WANT TO GO TO BED?

SO BEFORE IT ALL UNRAVELS.

WHY NOT DRINK YOUR GIN INSTEAD?

NELSON.

WHAT'S THE RUSH? WE HAVE ALL NIGHT.

I'VE STILL GOT MY APPETITE.

JOIN THE TABLE, IT EXTENDS.

HOW I LOVE A DINNER PARTY AT HOME WITH FRIENDS.

(to **ELLIE***)* Darling, I want to hear about all I missed.

ELLIE. *(looking for rescue)* It's been a busy busy summer. Susy!

SUSY. Well, um Nick has been writing. Nick, won't you tell us about your novel –

CORAL. Nick isn't a novelist. He's committed to – contextual excavation. That's why he's sailing to Greece –

NICK.

Ah ah – ARCHEOLOGY IS THRILLING

FINDING HIST'RY PETRIFIED.

CORAL.

NICK HAS SAID HE MIGHT BE WILLING

TO BECOME MY PRIVATE GUIDE.

NICK.

WHAT A JOKE! SHE'S SO MUCH FUN.

SHE'S INVITED EVERYONE

IT'S A TRIP SHE RECOMMENDS.

STREFFY.

HOW I LOVE A DINNER PARTY WITH ALL THESE 'FRIENDS'.

SUSY.

DO YOU THINK HE KNOWS? WHAT HE SHOULDN'T KNOW?

STREFFY.

JUST KEEP SMILING, DON'T LOOK GUILTY.

CORAL.

THESE ARE FAKE ANTIQUES.

NICK.

GOD I NEED A DRINK

ELLIE.

HELP ME THROUGH THIS

NICK. Ellie, you look marvelous. Sorry we haven't seen more of you. Where did you –

SUSY. – get that fabulous hat?

ELLIE. People who deny themselves things get warped and bitter, don't they?

CORAL. I agree. That's why I'm taking Nick to –

NICK. – to the beach.

STREFFY. And we're off to the Ball –

NICK. We?

STREFFY. I invited Susy.

NICK. What?

ALL. *(divided, overlapping)*

AREN'T YOU TIRED FROM YOUR TRAVELS?

DON'T YOU WANT TO GO TO BED?

SO BEFORE THIS ALL UNRAVELS

LET'S LEAVE ALL THE REST UNSAID.

STREFFY, SUSY.	NICK, CORAL, ELLIE, NELSON.
DO YOU THINK HE KNOWS?	LOOK AT HOW THE TIME HAS FLOWN
GOD, I NEED A DRINK.	I'D EAT OUT IF I HAD KNOWN
JUST KEEP SMILING,	THERE'S STILL TIME TO MAKE AMENDS
DON'T LOOK GUILTY.	
DO YOU THINK HE KNOWS?	
WHAT HE SHOULDN'T KNOW?	
YES WE DID IT.	

ALL.

> WITH A LOVELY DINNER PARTY AT HOME
> NOTHING LIKE A DINNER PARTY
> A CHARMING DINNER PARTY AT HOME....WITH....

NELSON. Stop! There's something you've neglected to tell me. *(beat)* Did you think I wouldn't notice? *(beat)* Wouldn't mind? *(beat)* Ellie! While a husband is away, a wife should never... – change the brand of his favorite gin!

ALL.

> FRIENDS!

> *(A car horn squawks.* **SUSY** *and* **STREFFY** *walk* **ELLIE** *and* **NELSON** *to the door.)*

SUSY. Goodbye Ellie! Have a safe trip!

STREFFY. Goodbye Old Nelson! Don't work too hard at the bank.

> *(***ELLIE** *and* **NELSON** *finally leave.)*

STREFFY. Well, my dear, we've seen it through.

SUSY. The poor dear does so like what she likes.

STREFFY. Can you believe she was with –

SUSY. *(covering her ears)* Don't tell me. What does it matter? They're gone. We're safe. I can look Nick in the eye again.

STREFFY. We can pretend this is ours again.

SUSY. She gave me this pretty jeweled bangle. I do like it – even knowing I'll exchange it for a month's rent somewhere.

STREFFY. Wear it tonight for the International Ball this evening. Let's get ready.

SUSY. Oh Streffy, I can't. I promised Nick I'd read his novel tonight.

STREFFY. *(He places the invitation on a table or the piano.)* Take the invitation. In case you change your mind.

> *(***STREFFY** *exits, following the others.* **SUSY** *exits the other way.)*

(**ELLIE** *comes running back in to find* **NICK**.)

ELLIE. Nick darling, there you are! I have something for you.

(*She hands him a jewelry box, and whispers loudly.*)

Thank you!

NICK. For what? For being so happy here?

ELLIE. For allowing me to be so happy elsewhere. You were such a good sport about the letters. And keeping things from Nelson. (*beat*) Why do you stare so? Didn't you know?

NICK. What are you talking about?

ELLIE. I will never forget your kindness. Goodbye!

(**ELLIE** *exits.* **NICK** *opens the box and takes out a pearl pin.*)

NICK. Susy!

(**SUSY** *enters happy, relieved.*)

SUSY. I'm ready to read! And then we'll celebrate, just the two of us.

NICK. Look what Ellie gave me!

SUSY. (*stalling*) It looks like a good pearl. She gave me this bracelet – isn't it pretty!

(**NICK** *tosses the box on the floor.*)

NICK. For what services exactly are we being so handsomely paid?

SUSY. Oh, it's just a trifle. For someone as wealthy as Ellie – it's like giving a pen-wiper.

NICK. The truth, Susy.

SUSY. I suppose she was grateful for our keeping up the house, watching over the servants.

NICK. She mentioned something about letters. And keeping something from Nelson. What is it my dear that you and I have been hired to hide from our host?

SUSY. What is it that Ellie said to you?

NICK. That's just what you'd like to know, isn't it, to know what line to take in making your explanation.

SUSY. Oh. Don't let us speak to each other like that!

NICK. Don't you see that we've got to have this thing out?

SUSY. I can't – not while you stand there like that. Nothing will do – as long as you're not you.

NICK. I haven't changed.

SUSY. You knew all about Ellie. Everyone used to talk about her adventures. Her tennis pros.

NICK. But that has nothing to do with us.

SUSY. I agree! It has nothing whatever to do with us.

NICK. Then what is the meaning of Ellie's gratitude, for what we've done?

SUSY. Not you.

NICK. Not me? Then you? Have you been mixed up in some dirty business of Ellie's? Answer me.

SUSY. Nelson wasn't supposed to know that she'd been away. She left me the letters to post once a week. I found them when we arrived. It was the price of our being here. Of all this. Oh Nick, please say it was worth it.

NICK. I would have refused.

SUSY. But you wanted to write here. You loved the view from your desk. Our being together depends on what we can get from other people. A little give and take. Haven't you ever –

NICK. No, I haven't. I've done menial jobs. I've lived in bad neighborhoods. But I won't do others dirty work for them.

SUSY. That's why I didn't tell you. So you could concentrate on your work.

NICK. Do you mean that this so called "give and take" is the price of our being together?

SUSY. Well, isn't it?

NICK. Then we'd better part. You were right. We're simply parasites. It won't do.

SUSY. But if the book's a success then…

NICK. What are the odds? And if it fails, what's the alternative? More lying? Just becoming used to it?

SUSY. But you needn't get involved. I'll manage everything.

NICK. I can't let you manage for me. I'm going out for a walk. Don't wait up!

SUSY. I won't!

(**NICK** *exits.* **SUSY** *suddenly notices the invitation Strefft left behind. She snatches up the invitation to the International Ball and reads aloud.*)

SUSY. *(cont.)* "The Twelfth Annual International Ball–"

SONG - CAN'T YOU HEAR THAT JAZZ?

SUSY. *(cont.)*

I CANNOT GO TO THIS PARTY.
HOW COULD I WALK THROUGH THAT DOOR?
WITH ALL THAT MUSIC AND DANCING AND GIN
I'M NOT THAT GIRL ANYMORE

THEY'LL BE PLAYING JAZZ
LIKE WE DANCED TOGETHER
AND THEY'LL WATCH ME DANCE ALONE.

SO SHOULD I GO TO THIS PARTY?
SAME PEOPLE IN A NEW PLACE?

(**STREFFY** *enters.*)

STREFFY. Are you coming or not?

SUSY/STREFFY.

A CAROUSEL OF A WORLD SPINNING ROUND.
YOU'VE GOT TO PICK UP THE PACE

CAN'T YOU HEAR THAT JAZZ?
CAN'T YOU HEAR IT PLAYING?
CAN'T YOU HEAR THAT JAZZ? DIVINE? DIVINE!

(*The party guests –* **ELLIE, URSULA, NELSON** *– enter and along with* **STREFFY,** *lure her into the dance.*)

ENSEMBLE (ELLIE, URSULA, NELSON, STREFFY)
    THERE'S ALWAYS ANOTHER PARTY,
    THERE'S ALWAYS ANOTHER SHOW
    CAN'T YOU HEAR THAT JAZZ…

    (dance break)

SUSY.	**ENSEMBLE ECHO**
SO I WILL GO TO THIS PARTY	CAN YOU HEAR THAT JAZZ?
THOUGH I DON'T WANT TO,	CAN YOU HEAR IT PLAYING?
I WILL.	
I'LL PAINT A SMILE,	
PUT A ROSE IN MY HAIR	CAN YOU HEAR THAT JAZZ?
I CAN'T AFFORD TO STAND	DIVINE!
STILL.	

SUSY.	**ENSEMBLE ECHO.**
CAN'T YOU HEAR THAT JAZZ?	CAN'T YOU HEAR THAT JAZZ?
CAN'T YOU HEAR IT PLAYING?	CAN'T YOU HEAR IT PLAYING?
CAN'T YOU HEAR THAT JAZZ?	CAN'T YOU HEAR THAT JAZZ?

ALL.
    DIVINE! DIVINE! DIVINE!

    *(Just before the end of the song, **NICK** appears in a spot-light, unseen, and observes **SUSY** surrounded by the mad bacchanal of the party.)*

    (blackout)

End of Act I

ACT II

Scene One
The Newport Regatta.
(August 1922 – The Next Day)

(NELSON, in captain's cap, beneath a line of sailing flags.)

NELSON. Ladies and Gentlemen, I am Commodore Nelson Vanderlyn. Welcome to the Newport Regatta, the highlight of the summer season. Of the favored boats leading today's race, three are owned by the same well-born family.

(NELSON demonstrates the race on top of the grand piano using large paper boats and toy buoys. Or a puppet show of boats on popsicle sticks, behind fabric waves. As he announces each boat he shows it to the audience.)

Sailing in *The Nereid* is Lord Arthur Strefford, the Earl of Altringham. *The Oxbow*, favorite for the America's Cup, is captained by the Earl's eldest, Harry Strefford. Harry's younger brother Phineas sails the *Phoenix* – his own ship – of his own design. The only member of the Altringham family not in the race today is the impecunious Winthrop Strefford.

The boats have to pass the buoys in the order indicated and navigate the tight turns back into port. The course today is a difficult one, especially in the present weather conditions. The meteorological report notes gusting winds and waves of almost hurricane height. Godspeed gentlemen.

(NELSON salutes the boats. The Sailing Race Music picks up.)

NELSON. *(cont.)* The race is on. Heading toward the first tight turn, close against the rocks, the three Altringham yachts are in the lead, with barely a length between them. And oh, the wind is fierce! *The Oxbow* is lifted practically out of the water – and in trying to avoid her, *The Nereid* has capsized, and the Phoenix is approaching much too fast! *The Oxbow* has come down but it appears to be rudderless! And here comes another giant wave. I can't look.

(As the music crashes and lightning flashes, all the boats are knocked over. **NELSON** *removes his cap and assumes a melodramatic tone as he addresses the audience and sings.)*

*(**SUSY, ELLIE, CORAL** and **STREFFY** enter in black as a funeral procession – carrying roses and black umbrellas.)*

SONG - TERRIBLE NEWS

NELSON.	**MOURNERS.**
TERRIBLE NEWS TODAY!	
OUT ON THE BAY	
THREE YACHTS RAN AGROUND.	
	– OOH!

NELSON.
TERRIBLE NEWS TODAY
FOR THEM WE PRAY,
SO MANY GOOD MEN WERE DROWNED.

                                        – AH!

AN AWFUL LOSS OF LIFE AND LIMB,
THE FAMILY'S FUTURE'S LOOKING GRIM

NELSON & MOURNERS.
WHAT AN AWFUL LOT OF TERRIBLE NEWS.

*(**STREFFY** dressed in black, steps out from the circle of mourners.)*

STREFFY.
TERRIBLE NEWS TODAY!
WHAT CAN I SAY?
A SHOCK SO PROFOUND

URSULA.

WHY??

STREFFY.

TERRIBLE NEWS TODAY!
OUT ON THE SPRAY
SHARKS ARE NOW CIRCLING ROUND

ELLIE.

AAAAH!

STREFFY.

AN AWFUL LOSS OF LIFE AND LIMB,
OF HIM AND HIM AND HIM AND – HMM...
LOOK AT WHAT I'VE GOT FROM TERRIBLE NEWS...

(With the sudden realization that his world has changed for the better, **STREFFY** *peels off his black mourning coat and catches a straw boater hat tossed by the band. He begins a frenetic celebratory dance to the suddenly fast music. Whenever the mourners see or address him, his tone is somber. But to the audience,* **STREFFY** *spins his umbrella and kicks his heels with glee.)*

STREFFY.

TERRIBLE NEWS TODAY
HIP HIP HOORAY!
FORTUNE'S WHEEL GOES AROUND.

TERRIBLE NEWS TODAY
GOOD MEN PASSED AWAY
THEY WERE LOST! I WAS FOUND!

ALL.

WERE THE FATES HERE TOO UNKIND?

STREFFY.

OR DID THEY ALL JUST READ MY MIND?

ALL.

WHAT AN AWFUL LOT OF TERRIBLE NEWS!

STREFFY.	**MOURNERS.**
MISFORTUNE FOR THEM,	– OOH – AH!
MEANS FORTUNE FOR ME.	– OOH – AH!
SO FROM NOW ON, I'M LIVING IN	
LUXURY!	

STREFFY.

TERRIBLE!

(Dance break, during which **STREFFY** *alternates between mourning with the others and breaking away to dance a gleeful jig.)*

ALL.

TERRIBLE NEWS TODAY!
WHAT A MELEE!
A LOSS OF RARE PEDIGREE!

TERRIBLE NEWS TODAY!
SO SAD TO SAY

STREFFY.

SO VERY NICE FOR ME!

ALL.

WE WATCHED THE RAGING WATERS SPIN.

STREFFY.

THEIR SHIPS WENT DOWN,
MY SHIP CAME IN!

OTHERS.

WHAT AN AWFUL LOT
OF TERRIBLE NEWS!
WE ARE ALL DISTRAUGHT!
FROM TERRIBLE NEWS!
WHAT A TRAGEDY!
WHAT TERRIBLE NEWS!

(Everyone exits, leaving **STREFFY** *alone on stage.)*

STREFFY.

JUST BETWEEN YOU AND ME –
NOT SUCH TERRIBLE NEWS!

(As the number buttons, the piano becomes a bar, and **STREFFY** *orders a double. Segue to next scene.)*

Scene Two
The Bar of the Newport Yacht Club

*(***NICK*** *enters – he's been out drinking, thinking – and makes his way over to* ***STREFFY****.)*

NICK. Streffy, I've been out all night. I just heard the news. I can't imagine how dreadful this must be for you. I'm so sorry for your loss.

STREFFY. My loss turns out to be my gain. My cousins' fatal fascination with yachting means that I am the new Earl of Altringham. Titled, propertied, rich. Drinks are on me.

NICK. You're really rich?

STREFFY. Loaded. Order champagne.

NICK. I mean, you can afford to marry now. Marry anyone.

STREFFY. You've already snagged the finest woman around, you lucky dog. *(pause)* Not forever, of course.

NICK. What?

STREFFY. How much longer do you think your "experiment" will continue?

NICK. We quarreled last night, but I figured out a way to make it work. We'll have a few more months, at least. Then I'll finish my novel, and we'll live simply.

STREFFY. And what of the future? I can't imagine Susy out of her setting of luxury and leisure. You should've seen her at the ball last night. Surrounded by princes and glittering jewels. She looked so very happy. *(beat)* She'd be better off with me…

NICK. With you?

STREFFY. After all, it's only a business deal until you each find a chance to "do better." I could give her – everything. Would you stand in her way?

SONG - I'LL STEP ASIDE

NICK.

DO I STILL ADORE HER?
AND WANT WHAT'S BEST FOR HER?
I JUST CAN'T IGNORE HER
LORD KNOWS I'VE TRIED

THOUGH I'LL ALWAYS LOVE HER
WON'T STOP THINKING OF HER.
BUT COULD I RECOVER?
TIME TO DECIDE...

LOVE HER? LEAVE HER?
SHE NEEDS A TAJ MAHAL
SHE'S THE TREASURE
BUT I HAVE NOTHING AT ALL

I LOVED HER BEFORE YOU
SO NOW I IMPLORE YOU
AND IF IT'S ME OR YOU
I'LL GIVE UP MY PRIDE.
I'LL STEP ASIDE, FOR YOU.

NICK.	**STREFFY.** (*echoing*)
LOVE HER!	LOVE HER!
KEEP HER!	KEEP HER!

NICK & STREFFY.

DRAPE HER IN SABLE FURS.
WEALTH AND PRIV'LEGE,
ALL THAT SHE DREAMS
    SHOULD BE HERS.

                              SHOULD BE HERS!

STREFFY.	**NICK.** (*echoing*)
SHE'S SOMEONE I CARE FOR	CARE FOR HER!
WOULD GO ANYWHERE FOR	MAKE HER LAUGH!

STREFFY & NICK. (*together*)

NEED A MILLIONAIRE FOR	NEED A MILLIONAIRE FOR
I COULD PROVIDE	YOU COULD PROVIDE
YOU'LL STEP ASIDE – FOR HER	I'LL STEP ASIDE – FOR HER

NICK. Our alliance was based on a moment's madness, and now the score must be paid. You have my blessing. Take good care of her.

(**NICK** *exits. Blackout.*)

Scene Three
The Barbizon Hotel in New York
(September 1922)

(In the lobby of a modest hotel for women, SUSY is on the telephone, speaking brightly, her enthusiasm a bit forced.)

SUSY. Ursula! Hello! It's Susy. Susy...Lansing. I'm at the Barbizon Hotel – just temporarily. I called to accept your invitation to stay at your Connecticut farm.... With your husband?!...No, Ursula – I won't! You'll have to find some other way to distract him. I am sorry to disappoint you, but I won't be able to visit after all.

(SUSY hangs up slowly and rings for the concierge.)

I'm afraid I don't have the rent yet...

(She removes the jeweled bracelet from her wrist and hands it over.)

Would you take this to the usual place and see what you can get for it?

(STREFFY appears in his new mourning attire, looking prosperous.)

STREFFY. Susy dear, what are you doing here in these dreary lodgings?

SUSY. Hello Streffy! Or should I say, your Lordship?

STREFFY. I'll still be Streffy, for you. He's better company than that dusty Earl. Tell me, how are you – and Nick?

SUSY. *(brightly, lying)* Wonderful! He's away – doing research on his book. I expect to hear from him any day...

STREFFY. Susy, dear. I'm the only person you don't need to lie to.

SUSY. I haven't heard from him. Why couldn't he ask me to go off somewhere with him and live like work-people do – in two rooms, without a servant?

STREFFY. I'd like to see you try to live in those two rooms without a servant. Why even in a palace, with a flock of shiny motors in the garage, most marriages fail.

SUSY. But I'm so young…. Life's so long. What does last then?

STREFFY. The hold of things we think we can do without. Habits, comforts, luxuries. They'll outlast the Pyramids. Happiness is a nice lunch, a good bottle of wine, a fine wristwatch.

SUSY. But surely there are people who live happily, meaningfully, without – nice things.

STREFFY. Yes – saints, heroes, hermits – all the fanatics. To which of these categories do we soft people belong?

SUSY. There must another choice.

STREFFY. Marry me, Susy.

SUSY. What? Please. Stop joking, Streff –

STREFFY. It's not Streff who's asking you now. The present offer comes from the Earl of Altringham, a British peer of independent means. Think it over my dear, as long as you like.

SUSY. I couldn't do that to Nick.

STREFFY. It was Nick's suggestion.

SUSY. Nick suggested it?!

STREFFY. He wants you to be happy.

SUSY. So he really does want to marry Coral. A writer needs leisure and luxury. I won't stand in his way.

STREFFY. While you're thinking over my offer, let me take you to a wonderfully extravagant dinner. I'll introduce you to my great aunt, the Duchess. And my new friend the Ambassador. I've become terribly popular, now that I'm rich.

SUSY. I don't have the right clothes to meet an Ambassador.

STREFFY. Order a new dress, an ermine cloak… A countess needs something splendid. Here's my card. Take it to Bergdorf's, and tell them to send me the bill.

(He removes a card from a silver case and hands it to her. As he exits, she remains standing, staring at the card.)

SUSY. *(reading the card)* Lord Winthrop Strefford of Altringham, Earl of North Umbrage...

(**SUSY** *sings* **CIGARS** *reprise.*)

SUSY.

SHOULD I BUY THE NEW DRESS?
BE A SOCIAL SUCCESS?
IN A FINE RESTAURANT
LIVE THE LIFE THAT I WANT –

WELL IT IS – MORE OR LESS.
A LIFE SURE TO IMPRESS
IF I TELL STREFFY, "YES"...
BUT A LIFE THAT'S NOT OURS...
OH, DAMN THOSE CIGARS!

(blackout)

Scene 4
The Fur Boutique of Bergdorf Goodman
(The Next Day)

(SUSY is comparing the furs on a few mannequins, delighted to be shopping for herself for the first time, rather than accompanying her wealthy friends. ELLIE enters and discovers SUSY there.)

ELLIE. Susy! What are you doing here in New York? I thought you were headed to the Gillow's place in Connecticut. Are you shopping for Ursula? If you mean to order that cloak for her I'd rather know.

SUSY. No. Today I am shopping for myself.

ELLIE. Yourself? Yourself! Surely Nick can't afford– a mahogany mink with a shantung silk lining!

SUSY. Nick and I mean to part – have parted, in fact. We simply decided that our situation was impossible.

ELLIE. Oh, oh! I didn't realize…that you were being… *(whispers loudly)* kept!

SUSY. Kept? Heavens, no!

(This is the first time she's telling anyone this.)

I've found someone proper to marry.

ELLIE. And you're choosing your trousseau! You lucky lucky girl! You clever clever darling! Who on earth is he?

SUSY. Streffy. Lord Strefford, Earl of Altringham

ELLIE. Streffy wants to marry you? My dearest, what a miracle of luck. Oh Susy, don't miss this chance. Marry him quickly.

SUSY. I'm not even divorced yet.

ELLIE. But why don't you announce your engagement at once. People do it now. It's so much safer. Engagement first, then divorce. Just follow my example.

(ELLIE waves her enormous engagement ring.)

SUSY. Ellie, why on earth would you ever leave poor Nelson?

ELLIE. I don't *want* to. I assure you, I simply hate it. But what am I to do? Algie is so rich, so impossibly rich, that other women keep throwing themselves at him.

SUSY. Algie?

ELLIE. Algie Bockheimer. I thought you knew.

SUSY. The one who made millions profiteering from government contracts during the war?

ELLIE. His money is a bit new. But so what? Nobody else in the world is as rich as the Bockheimers. I was with him – when I was so dreadfully happy – while you covered for me in Newport.

SUSY. How could you leave Nelson? With all your past together? I think you're abominable.

ELLIE. Abominable? Abominable, Susy?

SUSY. Yes, to ruin a perfectly good marriage, when you have all the money you could possibly want.

ELLIE. You're very cruel Susy. And quite naïve. You simply don't know what you're talking about. As if anybody ever had all the money they wanted!

(While **SUSY** *and* **ELLIE** *stare at each other coldly,* **CORAL** *enters and stands awkwardly near the door.)*

SUSY. Coral.

CORAL. Susy.

SUSY. You remember my friend Ellie Vanderlyn – from Newport. Coral Hicks.

ELLIE. Oh, you're the Bryn Mawr girl who came to dinner. You seemed overeducated. Genius is wasted on a woman who can't do a thing with her hair.

CORAL. Mrs. Vanderlyn, I hope you will let me return the favor, and invite you and Mr. Vanderlyn to Greece on our yacht. Mr. Lansing will be sailing with us. Susy, it was so kind of you to let me borrow your husband – his knowledge of the Ancient World is extraordinary. I may not give him back.

ELLIE. Susy, haven't you told her your news?

SUSY. No.

ELLIE. It's too wonderful. Susy is going to marry Lord Altringham. Our little Susy is going to be fantastically rich.

CORAL. It is indeed wonderful news.

SUSY. Isn't it? Enjoy the fox stole, Ellie – it suits you. Coral.

CORAL. Susy.

(**SUSY** *exits.*)

(**ELLIE***, eager for a new protégé and a new project, eyes* **CORAL.***)*

ELLIE. Coral, when *do* you leave for Greece?

CORAL. Well, um, Nick hasn't exactly committed…

ELLIE. I hope you won't mind my being candid. You simply must do something – about your – everything.

CORAL. I recognize the value of beauty in art and architecture, but it seems superficial to judge people by appearances.

ELLIE. Don't you want to be a success Coral?

CORAL. I'll never be graceful and witty like S– the way some people are so easily.

(**ELLIE** *circles around* **CORAL** *inspecting the raw materials of her new project.*)

SONG - THAT'S WHAT MONEY CAN BUY

ELLIE.
SO YOUR CLOTHING IS FUNNY
HELEN HAYES YOU ARE NOT.
THIS PROBLEM CAN BE REPAIRED
LIKE A BROKEN GREEK POT
You know those.

ELLIE.
FIRST GET RID OF THOSE GLASSES

CORAL. I need them to see!

ELLIE.
ADD A FUR AND BEHOLD
THE LIFE YOU WANT CAN BE YOURS,
IF YOU'VE GOT ENOUGH GOLD.

CORAL. Nick admires me for my intellect.

ELLIE. Darling, love isn't blind.

ELLIE.

> YOUR HAIR'S A MESS
> THIS SCARF WON'T DO
> YOU NEED A DRESS THAT FLATTERS YOU
> SO MUCH TO MODIFY
> THAT'S WHAT MONEY CAN BUY.
>
> YOUR SKIN IS MIXED
> YOUR FIGURE'S WORSE
> IT CAN BE FIXED
> YOU'VE GOT THE PURSE
> AN INFINITE SUPPLY
> THAT'S WHAT MONEY CAN BUY

CORAL.

> I WANT TO CLAIM A SCHOLAR AS MY LOVER.

ELLIE.

> HE'LL READ THE BOOK, ONCE YOU IMPROVE THE COVER.

CORAL.

> WHEN I MAKE ALL THESE CHANGES –

ELLIE.

> AND YOU GOTTA!

CORAL.

> – HE'LL VALUE ME MORE THAN ANCIENT TERRA COTTA.

(Transformation music. During the music, ELLIE teaches CORAL how to stand up straight, walk in heels, smile and dip alluringly. CORAL is a good student. In one smooth move, as ELLIE helps CORAL out of her break-away safari suit, a glittering flapper is revealed.)

CORAL.

> LOOK AT ME NOW
> I'LL KNOCK 'EM DEAD!
> ATHENA SPRUNG FROM ZEUS' HEAD
> WATCH ME TRANSMOGRIFY!

ELLIE.

> WEAR SOMETHING CHIC
> THIS IS MANHATTAN

CORAL. *agathos!*

ELLIE.

STOP SPEAKING GREEK.

CORAL.

I ALSO KNOW LATIN!

ELLIE & CORAL.

ON CASH YOU CAN RELY!
HERE'S WHAT MONEY CAN
THANK GOD MONEY CAN
THAT'S WHAT MONEY CAN BUY!

*(As **ELLIE** exits, she snatches away **CORAL**'s glasses, leaving her blinking.)*

Scene Five
Nick's Study & Susy's Hotel in New York
(October 1922 – Several Weeks Later)

(CORAL enters, showing off her new glamorous look.)

NICK. Coral!

CORAL. Hello – Nick?

(She tries to look seductive, but without her glasses can't really see.)

NICK. What did you do to yourself?

CORAL. I've been shopping. Isn't it grand?

NICK. You look…taller?

CORAL. I've been making preparations for Greece. And you?

NICK. I keep trying to work on my novel, but I've been so busy with the encyclopedia entries. I just handed in the last one. Z for Zakynthos.

CORAL. And you're wondering what to do next. Wondering what sort of employment could satisfy the demands of your superior mind.

NICK. Or just pay the rent.

CORAL. …I heard Susy is planning to marry Lord Altringham.

NICK. What?

(Meanwhile – STREFFY picks up SUSY for their date. SUSY wears a new fur, an evening gown and pearls. In the following scene, the STREFFY/SUSY conversation occurs at the same time, in a different location from NICK/CORAL.)

STREFFY. Don't people know by now that we are to be married?

SUSY. *(laughing)* No, they simply think you're giving me pearls and chinchilla cloaks.

STREFFY. With pleasure. Though I warn you the Altringham jewels are waiting for you in the vault.

SUSY. I can make Ellie crazy by wearing a different set every day.

CORAL. *(to* **NICK***)* Come to Greece – It's a real job, and a good salary.

NICK. Your eyes are...blue. I never noticed before.

SUSY. *(to* **STREFFY***)* It's all such a change!

STREFFY. And soon we'll be married –

CORAL. *(to* **NICK***)* You won't regret this.

NICK. Alright then, I accept.

STREFFY. *(to* **SUSY***)* – As soon as your divorce comes through.

CORAL. *(to* **NICK***)* I'm taking you out to celebrate –

SUSY. *(to* **STREFFY***)* Where are we dining tonight?

CORAL. *(to* **NICK***)* – Somewhere really elegant.

STREFFY. *(to* **SUSY***)* I think you'll like it.

STREFFY/CORAL. The Oak Room.

STREFFY. *(to* **SUSY***)* I'll check your fur.

(As they all exit, the lights darken.)

Scene Six
The Oak Room of the Algonquin Hotel in New York
(October 1922)

*(**NICK** and **SUSY** approach from different directions and spot each other in the restaurant.)*

SUSY. Nick!

NICK. Susy! What are you doing here?

SUSY. I'm dining with – Streffy. And you?

NICK. Coral. This is what you wanted isn't it?

SUSY. Of course. I hope you and Coral are equally content.

NICK. Perfectly.

SUSY. When you left Ellie's without saying goodbye, I assumed –

NICK. I had to leave Susy. I meant to write, but I couldn't –

SUSY. I hope your novel is going well.

NICK. I'm planning to write more this winter – in Greece. We're going away for six months.

SUSY. Yes, I heard – from Coral. What a wonderful opportunity for you. Really, how could you refuse?

NICK. Susy, are you happy?

SUSY. I'm happy for you, Nick. Happy you've found what really matters.

MUSICAL DIRECTOR. Ladies and Gentlemen, please take your seats.

NICK. But we're waiting for –

MUSICAL DIRECTOR. I am honored to welcome the crown prince/ss of cabaret, the sublime _____, *(the name of special guest)* to the Oak Room.

*(**SUSY** and **NICK** quickly sit down together at the nearest table.)*

*(**CABARET SINGER** enters to applause.)*

CABARET SINGER. It's wonderful to be back at the Oak Room. The most romantic room in New York. If you can't get the girl to say yes here, then, give up and go home. After all these years toiling in the velvet trenches, I can always spot the lovers.

(The **CABARET SINGER** *spots* **SUSY** *and* **NICK**.*)*

CABARET SINGER. Oh, we've got the real thing here tonight. A young couple in love.

NICK. I assure you, you're mistaken.

SINGER. You're practically still on your honeymoon.

SUSY. We were together, once. But that's all over now. We've both found more appropriate partners.

SINGER. You say that so confidently. I used to feel that way too, a long time ago.

(The song is sung to the audience, but **SUSY** *and* **NICK** *listen intently. During the song, they steal glances at each other and then slowly reach across the table to hold hands.)*

SONG - RIGHT HERE, RIGHT NOW

CABARET SINGER.

I THOUGHT THAT I'D BE YOUNG FOREVER.
I THOUGHT I'D ALWAYS HAVE MORE TIME
I THOUGHT I'D HAVE A THOUSAND CHANCES...
WHAT WAS I WAITING FOR?

I THOUGHT THAT I HAD ALL THE ANSWERS
I'D KNOW WHEN LOVE WALKED THROUGH MY DOOR
WITH BRIGHT BOUQUETS AND MOONLIT DANCES
BUT STILL I WANTED MORE –

DON'T WASTE A SINGLE SUMMER DAY,
DON'T LET YOUR TRUE LOVE SLIP AWAY.
RIGHT HERE, RIGHT NOW. START.
JUST LISTEN. BEAT HEART.
INSTEAD OF WONDERING WHAT MIGHT HAVE BEEN –
RIGHT HERE, RIGHT NOW, BEGIN.

CABARET SINGER. *(cont.)*

    YOU LOOK SO SMART AND OH SO CERTAIN
    THE WAY I WAS, MY WHOLE LIFE LONG.
    SO SURE MY DREAMS WOULD STILL BE WAITING,
    TURNS OUT THAT I WAS WRONG.

    AND NOW IT'S HARDER TO BE HOPEFUL
    SO MUCH I WISH I'D NEVER SAID
    DON'T COUNT ON WHAT YOU'LL DO TOMORROW,
    WHO KNOWS WHAT LIES AHEAD?
    SEE WHAT'S RIGHT HERE INSTEAD.

    (By this point, **NICK** *and* **SUSY** *are holding hands, looking at each other.)*

    DON'T LEAVE WITH JUST A BACKWARD GLANCE,
    DON'T HOLD OUT FOR A BETTER CHANCE,
    RIGHT HERE – AND RIGHT NOW!

    DON'T CLOSE YOUR EYES TO ALL THAT LIES WITHIN
    RIGHT HERE
    RIGHT NOW
    BEGIN!

    (Amid applause, the **CABARET SINGER** *bows and exits.)*

    *(***NICK*** is still holding* **SUSY***'s hand.)*

NICK. Let's give it another try.

SUSY. We still have the carving set and the grape scissors.

    (As they contemplate running off together, **STREFFY** *enters with* **SUSY***'s fur.* **CORAL** *approaches from the other side. There is a long awkward moment as* **STREFFY** *sizes up the situation. He won't back off.)*

STREFFY. Our table is waiting.

    *(***NICK*** and* **SUSY** *look at each other for a long beat. Finally,* **SUSY** *pulls away from* **NICK** *and takes her fur from* **STREFFY***.)*

NICK. Congratulations, Susy. You'll be a marvelous countess.

SUSY. It would be best for us both to have our liberty. Don't you agree?

NICK. I'll have my lawyer send you the divorce papers.

SUSY. Goodbye Nick.

(SUSY *and* NICK *shake hands coolly.* SUSY *and* STREFFY *exit.* NICK *and* CORAL *sit down at the table as the lights come down.*)

Scene Seven
Outside Ellie's Brownstone
(April 1923)

*(Reprise of opening **MODERN AGE** music – instrumental)*

(A much-changed **NELSON** *makes his way down the street, scat singing to the music, drinking from a flask.* **NELSON** *is in mid-life crisis, trying desperately to look young and modern.* **SUSY**, *dressed in white, on her way to her engagement party, runs into him.)*

SUSY. Nelson!

NELSON. Well, well, aren't you the bees knees! Glad to see you Susy, my dear.

SUSY. You too, Nelson.

NELSON. Caught you at it, eh? Have you been away all this time?

SUSY. No. I'm in town.

NELSON. Me too, taking care of this divorce business. Everything's Jake, right? Copacetic.

SUSY. I must say, you're taking it well.

NELSON. Got to keep up with the times, eh? Let that hot-house flower out! I'm all for new sensations, aren't you my dear? Care to go dancing? I know a jive joint.

SUSY. I'm sorry Nelson, I'm late for –

NELSON. Great thing, this liberty! Everything's changed nowadays, why shouldn't marriage too? Show me where it says in the Bible, though shalt not divorce. Moses left it out because he knew about human nature. Live and let live, eh?

SUSY. That's very modern of you.

NELSON. I hear you're following our example yourself. First rate idea. I don't mind telling you I saw it coming – when you were with us at Newport. Caught you at it, so to speak. Old Nelson isn't as blind as people think. I've got a flask. Let's toast to the health of Streff and Mrs. Streff.

SUSY. I hope our marriage will last even longer that you and – .

NELSON. Do you ever talk to her?

SUSY. Sometimes. I'm on my way to your – I mean, her house now. Would you like to come with me?

NELSON. Oh. No. But, please when you see her, tell her I'm happy.

(Throughout the song NELSON *persists in trying to convince* SUSY *– and himself – that he is in fact happy. While the tone is slightly forced, he preserves the lie until the very last line.)*

SONG - TELL HER I'M HAPPY

NELSON. *(cont.)*

TELL HER I'M FINE
I'LL NEVER FORGET HER
BUT I'M NOT GOING TO FIGHT
I'M PERFECTLY EXACTLY ALL RIGHT

TELL HER I'M SPLENDID
TELL HER I'M SWELL.
THOUGH OTHERS MAY JUDGE HER
I WON'T EVER COMPLAIN
I'M CAPITAL, I'M RIGHT AS RAIN

WHEN YOU SEE HER –
TELL HER I'M FREE NOW
TELL HER I'VE GROWN
TELL HER I'M MUCH BETTER OFF ON MY OWN

TELL HER I'M BUSY
CAN'T SLEEP AT ALL
TOO MANY PARTIES, TO EVEN RECALL.

(As the music swells, NELSON *lifts* SUSY *up and twirls her around).*

TELL HER I'M GLAD
TELL HER I'M PLEASED
SHE'S RETURNED TO HER YOUTH.
TELL HER ANYTHING
TELL HER ANYTHING!

(He tries to get past **SUSY** *before he breaks down into sobs.)*

NELSON. *(cont.)*

JUST DON'T TELL HER THE TRUTH.

*(***NELSON*** *raises his flask and exits.)*

*(***SUSY***, shaken, continues on to* **ELLIE**'s *brownstone, now set up for a party.)*

Scene Eight
Inside Ellie's Manhattan Brownstone
& Outside the Hotel Nouveau Luxe

(**ELLIE**'s *party in full swing. The band plays an instrumental reprise of* **MODERN AGE**. *There is the option to have* **ELLIE** *and* **STREFFY** *sing this reprise to set the top of the scene.* **ELLIE** *wears a sparkling evening gown.* **SUSY** *wears bridal white.*)

ELLIE. Susy, I am so glad you agreed to put aside our differences and let me throw you an engagement party. I always like to throw a party on April 23rd.

SUSY. Isn't it your anniversary?

ELLIE. Well yes, it was. But, I've moved on. As you've discovered, there's no profit in sentimentality.

SUSY. I ran into Nelson on my way here. He's –

ELLIE. How is the old dear? Come, let me introduce you to my little Algie.

SUSY. Ellie, aren't you the least bit uncomfortable about flaunting him to all your friends? Friends who wanted nothing to do with the Bockheimers. Or friends who might be loyal to Nelson?

ELLIE. Well, if anyone is going to be old-fashioned and moralistic on me, they won't get invited on Algie's yacht. Come on Susy. We're all modern now. (*looking offstage*) No, no! The champagne goes on the left!

(**ELLIE** *exits,* **STREFFY** *approaches. He is more formal, not fun anymore.*)

STREFFY. Susan, there you are –

SUSY. I just saw Nelson outside – he's a wreck.

STREFFY. Poor old 'Caught you at it'. Never caught what was going on under his nose.

SUSY. Can you believe Ellie was dallying with Bockheimer for all that time while we were in Newport!

STREFFY. Of course, I knew dear. Where do you think Ellie and he were cavorting? In my fishing camp – the scene of the famous honeymoon.

SUSY. My honeymoon nest amid the rosebushes!

STREFFY. I must say Bockheimer paid a thumping good rent for that cottage.

SUSY. How could you?!

STREFFY. How could *you?!* None of this would have happened without your mailing Ellie's letters in the first place.

SUSY. Oh Streffy!

STREFFY. Susan dear. In public, from now on, please make an effort to call me Winthrop.

SUSY. Winthrop!

STREFFY. It is my given name. And people look to me now, to set an example, the proper tone and so forth. Especially when we take up residence in Altringham.

SUSY. I didn't realize we'd have to –

STREFFY. We can travel of course, go to London, but I'll have to oversee the estate, the farms. It's my responsibility. But you'll be living in a castle, my countess.

(He puts his arm around **SUSY** *and pulls her close, painting the romantic scene.)*

From one of the towers, there's a magical view of the moon as it rises over the lake...

*(***STREFFY*** tries to kiss her.* **SUSY** *has never felt any physical attraction towards him and she pulls away, startled.* **STREFFY** *takes it in stride. He's disappointed, but not deterred.)*

I'll be waiting for you my countess – we'll spend the rest of our lives together.

*(***STREFFY*** exits.)*

*(***SUSY,*** miserable, walks down the "aisle" toward her future.)*

SONG - BUT YOU'RE NOT HIM

SUSY.

THIS IS THE LIFE I HOPED TO LEAD
THESE ARE THE GAMES I USED TO CARE FOR
ALL OF THESE THINGS I USED TO NEED
I NO LONGER KNOW WHAT THEY ARE THERE FOR.

(Lights fade on Susy and rise on the street outside the Hotel Nouveau Luxe. The Hicks have returned from their cruise, and are back in New York. A well-dressed **CORAL** *triumphantly leads a cowed* **NICK***. He is carrying her souvenirs and packages, while she looks through the mail.)*

CORAL. The wonderful thing about New York is that you can go away to Greece for six months and absolutely nothing has changed. Look at a newspaper. Same headlines. Same social gossip. Oh, there's a letter for you.

(While **CORAL** *blathers,* **NICK** *scans the newspaper for news of* **SUSY***'s engagement to* **STREFFY***. When he finds the notice about her party, he drops* **CORAL***'s packages.)*

CORAL. What is it?

NICK. Susy's getting married to Altringham – there's a party today.

CORAL. When are we getting married?

NICK. What?

CORAL. Come along Nick, I don't want to be late for varnishing day at the Gallery. Daddy said he'd buy us a Picasso.

*(***CORAL** *exits.)*

NICK.

THIS PRIV'LEGED LIFE WITH ALL THE FRILLS,
IT'S AWFULLY HARD TO BE OBJECTIVE
THERE IS A PRICE FOR ALL THOSE THRILLS.
I'M NO LONGER SURE OF MY PERSPECTIVE.

(Lights reveal **SUSY** *and* **NICK** *in their separate worlds.)*

NICK.   **SUSY.**

    WHAT CAN I SAY?

    YOU ARE NOT HER   YOU ARE NOT HIM

    HOW CAN I STAY   HOW CAN I STAY?

    WHEN YOU'RE NOT HER?

SUSY.

    WHAT IS LEFT OF SOUL I WONDER?

NICK.

    WHAT IS LEFT OF ART?

NICK & SUSY.

    WHAT USE KNOWING LOVE AT LAST – NOW THAT WE'RE
        APART?

    CAUGHT UP IN THIS MASQUERADE. WE WERE OH SO SMART.

    KNOWING HOW THE GAME WAS PLAYED. NOW WE'RE APART.

NICK.   **SUSY.**

    IN EVERY WAY,   ALL OF THE LIES THIS LIFE
                            ENTAILS

    YOU ARE NOT HER   THE LITTLE WAYS ONE
                            HURTS AND FLATTERS

                            NO MATTER HOW YOU TRY,
                            IT FAILS

                            YOU CAN'T ATTAIN WHAT
                            REALLY MATTERS.

NICK & SUSY.

    THIS IS THE DAY I DREAMED ABOUT

    THIS IS THE GIRL /MAN I THOUGHT I WANTED

    HOW CAN I SAY, I'VE CHANGED MY MIND

    BY MIGHT HAVE BEENS, I AM STILL HAUNTED.

SUSY.

    SQUINT ONE EYE

    BUT YOU'RE NOT HIM

    I WILL GET BY

    BUT YOU'RE NOT HIM.

SUSY & NICK.

    I WILL GO ON

    THOUGH YOU'RE NOT HIM/HER.

    MY LOVE IS GONE

    AND YOU'RE NOT HIM/HER !

(Lights down on **NICK**. *He exits.)*

(As the song ends, **STREFFY** *and* **ELLIE** *enter for the toast.)*

STREFFY. To my bride, the future Countess of North Umbridge, Susan Strefford –

SUSY. Lansing. I'm Susy Lansing.

ELLIE. *(to* **SUSY**) Shh!

SUSY. Streffy – Winthrop – I can't go through with it. I'm sorry.

(Furious, **STREFFY** *stalks off.)*

ELLIE. Have you gone mad or are you just stupid?

SUSY. I have to leave.

ELLIE. What will I say to everyone?

SUSY. What you told me back in Newport. That we were meant to be…happy. I finally understand. I've got to tell Nick.

ELLIE. *(**ELLIE**'s cold ambition melts for just a moment.)* Happy? Happy? I lack your courage Susy.

*(**ELLIE** gulps her champagne.)*

I didn't intend to tell you, but Nick is back in New York. I read in the paper that he and Coral returned today.

SUSY. Nick is here! Where?

ELLIE. Algie's motor car is outside. Tell his driver to take you to the Hotel Nouveau Luxe.

*(**SUSY** kisses **ELLIE** and runs off. **ELLIE** exits.)*

Scene Nine
Outside the Hotel Nouveau Luxe

SUSY. Nick!

(SUSY rushes in, looking for NICK. Her urgency is not about trying to lure him back, but rather her eagerness to share her own exhilaration at finally feeling free of society. SUSY has come to despise the selfish and manipulative world that ELLIE and STREFFY represent. Having discovered this truth about herself, she wants to apologize for her earlier behavior. But NICK is gone.)

(As SUSY tries to twist off Streffy's engagement ring. NICK returns and walks toward her.)

NICK. Congratulations to the bride.

SUSY. I don't deserve any congratulations. I was becoming someone I didn't want to be. Worse than a parasite. A perpendicular person – with no compassion. I wish I had your moral clarity, your strength. Coral is very fortunate. I wish you happiness, Nick.

NICK. Are you going to London now?

SUSY. No.

NICK. Streff's castle?

SUSY. No. I couldn't. I couldn't do it Nick.

NICK. So you're not –

SUSY. I'm going to look for a job as a governess. In the country, away from everyone I know.

NICK. Why Susy?

SUSY. I couldn't marry Streff.

NICK. My novel's been accepted by Knopf. They've sent me a whopping advance.

(He removes a folded check from his pocket and hands it to her.)

SUSY. One hundred dollars! How wonderful for you. Coral must be pleased.

NICK. Coral didn't care. *(pause)* Will you marry me?

SUSY. What? What about Coral?

NICK. She's not you.

SUSY. I can't imagine being married to anyone else.

(They embrace.)

NICK. Wait! Has our divorce gone through?

SUSY. *(a beat)* We're still married!

NICK. But if Ellie wants to throw another party…

SUSY. This time, we'll keep the gifts!

(As the moonlight floods in, they sing a reprise of **GLIMPSES OF THE MOON**.*)*

SUSY & NICK.

WHAT A LUXURY WE SHARE,
NOW OUR LIFE CAN START ANEW.
AND IT'S FREE TO DREAM AND DARE
I AM RICH WHEN I'M WITH YOU.
WE'LL BUILD CASTLES IN THE AIR

I'D BE SATISFIED WITH STARLIGHT,
AS LONG AS YOU ARE THERE.

EVERY THING YOU'RE DREAMING OF!
SO NOW WE'LL GET BY ON NOTHING
MORE THAN LOVE.
CLOUDS MAY FILL THE SKY TOO SOON
BUT WE'LL ALWAYS HAVE OUR GLIMPSES OF THE MOON.

The End

Curtain Call Reprise

(After the cast has bowed, all – including the **CABARET SINGER** *– sing a reprise of* ***MODERN AGE.****)*

ALL.
AINT WE GOT FUN!
SOMETHING FOR EVERYONE
LATE NIGHT CABARETS
BEING RICH REALLY PAYS
IN SO MANY WAYS
LIVING IN THIS MODERN –
    THE COUNTRY'S DRY; CHAMPAGNE IS DRIER.
    THE MARKET'S HIGH, WE'RE GETTING HIGHER
– AGE!
WELCOME TO THIS MODERN AGE!

PROPERTIES

ACT I

Scene 1
Long necklace (gift for Ellie)
6 champagne glasses
champagne bottle
$20 check, folded
bridal veil
bouquet
top hat
gift-wrapped wedding presents

Scene 2
Trunk
Small notebook/calendar
fountain pen
Cigar box
Cigar
crystal lighter
silver candlesticks
crystal vase
additional wrapped gifts

Scene 3
Suitcase for Susy
pink note
packet of sealed letters, tied with ribbon
pencil
purse
wrapped gift box (footed compote)
typewriter
blank typing paper
typewriter ribbon
large envelope – from Arthur Murray Dance Studio
3 colored, numbered footprints
business card – Knopf
Letter – from Ellie to Nelson
typed manuscript pages
suitcase for Coral
archeology field bag
pottery fragment with Greek inscription and art
invitation to the International Ball
travelling case – Ellie's
jeweled bracelet – Ellie's gift for Susy
cocktail glass with gin
jewelry gift box
pearl tie pin

ACT II

Scene 1
Regatta flags
Captain's cap
3 toy or paper sailing yachts (these can be real or just photographs of
boats glued to foam core.)
2 buoys (1 red, I green battery-operated candle)
rocks
black umbrellas
3 long-stem roses
straw boater hat

Scene 2
Telephone
concierge bell
silver card case
calling card, "Lord Winthrop Strefford"

Scene 3
mannequins draped with furs
huge diamond engagement ring for Ellie

Scene 6
flask – Nelson

Scene 7
mail
newspaper
champagne glasses
$100 check, folded

COSTUME PLOT

ACT I

Scene 1: The Vanderlyn Brownstone

STREFFY
Blue/White Seersucker suit
White checkered shirt
Cufflinks
Striped Socks
Blue Sweater Vest
Yellow/Navy bowtie

NICK
Baby yellow shirt
Tan vest
Gold/Blue striped tie
Tan linen jacket
Butterscotch pocket square
Pin stripe linen pants

NELSON
White tux shirt
Tux pants
Bow Tie
Cummerbund
White Jacket
Black Socks
Black Shoes

ELLIE
Peach dress
Pearls
Silver Shoes
White/Peach/pearl earrings
Rhinestone bracelet

SUSY
Light blue satin dress
Ivory shoes
Long white gloves

URSULA
Geometric print dress
Turban
Black shoes
Black gloves
Geometric bracelet
Teardrop earrings

Scene 2: Streffy's Fishing Camp in Maine

STREFFY

Remove seersucker jacket and bowtie
Add red vest, red bowtie, red smoking jacket

NICK

Remove jacket and tie
Add gold vest, paisley tie, blue stripe jacket

SUSY

White/Blue Sailor top
Navy skirt

Scene 3: Ellie's Newport Mansion:

ELLIE

For "Letters"
White dress
White Lace Gloves
Silver Shoes

For "Letter to Nelson #3"
Purple/pink lingerie shorts
Purple/pink lingerie top

For "Dinner Party with Friends"
Green dress with feathers
Red/gold striped jacket
Gold head band
Gold shoes

NELSON

"Dinner Party With Friends"
Remove ALL
Add gray pants, white/red striped shirt, navy jacket, navy/red striped tie

NICK

For Scene 3
Remove jacket and tie
Add white sweater

For "Writing Montage"
Remove sweater and tie

For "Glories of Greece"
Blue tie
Tan vest
Tan jacket
Navy pocket square

SUSY

"Letters to Nelson #2"
Remove Sailor top
Add beige top

"Letters to Nelson #4"
Remove ALL
Add light blue satin dress

After "Dinner Party With Friends"
Remove blue satin dress
Add orange beaded dress

MAID

"Letters to Nelson"
Black/white dress
Black/white wide maid's headband
Black Mary Jane Heels
White Apron

CORAL

"Glories of Greece"
Brown lace up shoes
Tan polka dot shirt
Tan sweater vest
Tan skirt suit
Glasses

STREFFY

"Glories of Greece"
Remove ALL except shirt
Add Light blue pants, tennis sweater, and yellow/navy bowtie, white cap

"Dinner Party With Friends"
Remove sweater, bowtie and cap
Add seersucker jacket, blue vest, and pink/blue bowtie

ACT TWO
Scene 1: The Newport Regatta

STREFFY
Seersucker suit
Pink shirt
Cufflinks
Navy/Silver/pink bowtie
Boater hat
Black trench coat

NICK
Same as "Greece"
Remove jacket

NELSON
Remove jacket, shirt
Add blue shirt, blue sweater vest, ascot, captain's cap

ELLIE
Black shirt
Black skirt
Black hat
Black shoes

CORAL (as mourner)
"Maid's" dress (backwards)
Black hat
Black shoes
Long black jacket
Black gloves

SUSY (as mourner)
Black hat
Black coat
Black shoes

Scene 3: the Barbizon Hotel

SUSY
Floral print dress
jeweled bracelet

STREFFY
Add silk scarf

Scene 4: Bergdorf's Fur Boutique

ELLIE
Light purple/pink bias dress
Knee-length crocheted sweater
Silver shoes
White hat

SUSY
   Add: knee-length jacket
   Cloche hat

CORAL
   Underdress:
   Transformation dress
   Multi-colored pearls
   Floral pumps
   Overdress:
   Safari suit
   Colorful scarf
   Brown lace up shoes
   Glasses

Scene 5 and Scene 6: The Oak Room

STREFFY
   Remove ALL
   Add tuxedo shirt, tuxedo pants, black bowtie, black/grey dotted vest

NICK
   Remove shirt
   Add navy jacket, cufflinks, tan vest, blue shirt/French cuffs, blue tie,
   cream pocket square

SUSY
   Peach satin evening dress
   White fur stole
   Long pearls
   Long white gloves
   Pearl bracelet

Scene 7: Outside Ellie's Brownstone

NELSON
   Remove pants, vest, ascot
   Add white pinstripe suit, long scarf

SUSY
   Remove peach dress, fur stole
   Add white long dress, white cape

Scene 8: Inside Ellie's Brownstone/Outside Hotel Nouveau Luxe

ELLIE
   Silver beaded dress
   Silver shoes
   Chandelier earrings
   Blingy necklace
   Top of show bracelet
   Engagement ring

STREFFY

Add silk sash, medals

CORAL

French vanilla dress
Gold scarf
Pearl earrings
Pearl/gold necklace
Brocade purse
Floral pumps
Beaded headband
NO glasses

Scene 9: Finale

NICK

Remove Greek cap

Set design by Daniel Pinha for the 2010 production at MetroStage in Alexandria, VA.

OTHER TITLES AVAILABLE FROM SAMUEL FRENCH

SHINE!: THE HORATIO ALGER MUSICAL

Book by Richard Seff
Music by Roger Dean Anderson
Lyrics by Lee Goldsmith

13m, 6f / Various sets.

**Winner! 2010 New York Musical Theatre Festival
Award for Excellence
Winner! National Music Theatre Network Award!**

This charming rags to riches romp with a melodic score follows Ragged Dick, Horatio Alger's first best selling hero, from penniless bootblack to budding Wall Street entrepreneur. His adventures bring him face to face with scheming ex convicts, vicious comic villains, kind benefactors and a world of colorful street characters. Set in the New York Centennial summer of 1876, this full of hopes and dreams musical is perfect for the whole family.

"A charming, feel-good musical. The work's tremendous heart and unabashed celebration of Alger's popular stories are in ample evidence in this appealing musical about the rise from rags to riches."
– Meredith Lee, *Theatermania*

"*SHINE!* is one of those wonderful musicals where an audience cares deeply for the hero. Richard Seff's book and Lee Goldsmith's lyrics perfectly capture the Horatio Alger spirit ...Composer Roger Anderson's ballads are strikingly beautiful. As for his up-tempo songs, to call each a toe-tapper would only be 10% accurate: every one is a TOES-tapper."
– Peter Filichia, *The Star-Ledger*

"Awfully close to the sort of musical that made the form nationally beloved in the Rodgers and Hammerstein era."
– Marc Miller, *Backstage*

SAMUELFRENCH.COM

OTHER TITLES AVAILABLE FROM SAMUEL FRENCH

AMERICAN TALES

Book and Lyrics by Ken Stone
Music by Jan Powell

Musical in two acts, based on stories
by classic American writers

Musical in two acts, based on stories by classic American writers / 4m, 1f / Period costumes and set pieces, mid to late 19th century

Ovation Award nomination for Best Book/Lyrics/Music
Kleban Award winner, Libretto *(Bartleby, the Scrivener)*

Act I, *The Loves of Alonzo Fitz Clarence and Rosannah Ethelton*, is from Mark Twain's story of two people falling in love at a great distance with the aid of that brand-new invention, the telephone. Alonzo in Maine and Rosannah in California meet by the accident of crossed wires and each falls in love with an imagined ideal of the other. So complete is their self-deception that even when brought face to face they cannot recognize each other. Love is found, lost, and found again. Played as period melodrama, but the relevance to 21st century dating habits is clear.

Act II, *Bartleby, the Scrivener*, is dramatized from Herman Melville's slyly funny but ultimately tragic story. Building on the theme of human connections made and missed, this act takes a darker turn, looking at people who occupy the closest of quarters and yet don't really communicate at all. Bartleby, employed as a copyist in a law office of the 1840s, inexplicably begins to refuse to work, forcing his colleagues to ask themselves the transforming question that ends the play: What do we owe to the people who come into our lives?

"Excellent new musical."
– Critic's Choice, *The Los Angeles Times*

OTHER TITLES AVAILABLE FROM SAMUEL FRENCH

HAPPY NEW YEAR

Adapted by Bert Shevelove
Songs by Cole Porter

14m, 11f (doubling possible.) / Var. ints. (may be simply suggested)

This clever show has given new life to one of America's most popular comedies. The story concerns an eager young man who falls in love with the wrong rich girl. In the final scene he realizes that it is her young, unconventional sister whom he really loves, and the two turn their backs on old money and old values for a shared life that should prove to be a holiday.

"Mr. Shevelove has matched Barry's happy go lucky book with a fountain of effervescent Porter tunes."
– *The New York Times*

"A playful, tuneful, civilized musical."
– *New York Post*

OTHER TITLES AVAILABLE FROM SAMUEL FRENCH

27 RUE DE FLEURUS
(MY LIFE WITH GERTRUDE)

Ted sod & Lisa Koch

5f / Musical / Unit Set

Unlike most of the stage works about Gertrude and Alice, *27 Rue de Fleurus* is told from Alice's point of view. Gertrude grows tired of Alice's lack of panache for telling her perspective of their story and attempts to hijack the play as only the author of such lines as "sugar is not a vegetable" can. But Alice has secrets to share with the audience that silence the famously verbose Gertrude. This celebrated couple confronts each other about love, marriage, jealousy, genius and a few other delicious topics while Pablo Picasso, F. Scott Fitzgerald, Mabel Dodge, Sylvia Beach and even Jean Harlow drop by for a visit.

"*27 Rue de Fleurus* gets its sweetness from a genuine love of its subject, the "marriage" of Gertrude Stein and Alice B. Toklas. The music is well handled by John Bell; and the all-female cast sings excellently."
– *The Village Voice*

"What we have here is a love story, fraught with jealousy and passion like others, but most of all, it celebrates the incredible bond between two women who decided to share their lives, even during a time when it was relatively unheard of. That alone makes *27 Rue de Fleurus* worth an evening of your time."
– *GO Magazine*

"Ms. Rosenblat, who, seated, resembles portraits of Stein, plays Gertrude as a commanding bully. And Ms. Stern's Alice is a bright, attractive creature. ("Everyone is entitled to a bit of fantasy," she says.) They're strong, plausible performances."
– *The New York Times*

OTHER TITLES AVAILABLE FROM SAMUEL FRENCH

ADRIFT IN MACAO

Book and Lyrics by Chirstopher Durang
Music by Peter Melnick

Full Length, Musical / 4m, 3f / Unit Sets

Nominated for a Drama Desk Award for Best Music

Set in 1952 in Macao, China, *Adrift in Macao* is a loving parody of film noir movies. Everyone that comes to Macao is waiting for something, and though none of them know exactly what that is, they hang around to find out. The characters include your film noir standards, like Laureena, the curvaceous blonde, who luckily bumps into Rick Shaw, the cynical surf and turf casino owner her first night in town. She ends up getting a job singing in his night club – perhaps for no reason other than the fact that she looks great in a slinky dress. And don't forget about Mitch, the American who has just been framed for murder by the mysterious villain McGuffin. With songs and quips, puns and farcical shenanigans, this musical parody is bound to please audiences of all ages.

"And there are of course those songs… Melnick demonstrates an affinity for melody and old-fashioned showmanship that link him to his grandfather, Richard Rodgers…"
– Matthew Murray, *TalkinBroadway.com*

"… with a drop-dead funny book and shamefully silly lyrics by Chirstopher Durang and lethally catchy music by Peter Melnick. *Adrift In Macao* lovingly parodies the Hollywood film noir classics of the 1940's and 50's…"
– Michael Dale, *Broadwayworld.com*

CPSIA information can be obtained
at www.ICGtesting.com
Printed in the USA
FSOW04n1100280916
25502FS